She was her father's daughter, all right.

She looked so like him. She shared the same tainted blood. Women like her were good for one thing only....

His senses flared as he looked at her again. With that in mind, he would have to build a few bridges. Didn't they say revenge was a dish best served cold? Though when they got between the sheets he'd take his hot. Little Sophie Ford had ripened like a peach for the plucking—and he was developing quite an appetite.

RED HOT REVENGE

There are times in a man's life...

when only seduction will settle old scores!

Pick up our exciting series of revenge-based
romances—they're recommended and red-hot!

Available only from
Harlequin Presents®

Susan Stephens

THE SPANIARD'S REVENGE

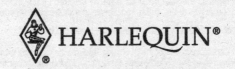

HARLEQUIN®

TORONTO • NEW YORK • LONDON
AMSTERDAM • PARIS • SYDNEY • HAMBURG
STOCKHOLM • ATHENS • TOKYO • MILAN • MADRID
PRAGUE • WARSAW • BUDAPEST • AUCKLAND

For Sara, James and Leonie. I love you.

ISBN 0-373-12389-2

THE SPANIARD'S REVENGE

First North American Publication 2004.

Copyright © 2004 by Susan Stephens.

This edition published by arrangement with Harlequin Books S.A.

® and TM are trademarks of the publisher. Trademarks indicated with
® are registered in the United States Patent and Trademark Office, the
Canadian Trade Marks Office and in other countries.

Visit us at www.eHarlequin.com

Printed in U.S.A.

PROLOGUE

THE man lounging back on the pale hide sofa appeared infinitely more at ease than the camera crew and reporters crowding the room. But he was suffering the glare of the lights, and people from Wardrobe were still buzzing around him like gnats.

As he sent a look spinning up to dismiss them, one girl holding a fat brush loaded with powder misread the signs and froze, trapped in his stare. Her eyes darkened and her lips plumped, all within the space of a few seconds. The television lights were blindingly bright but, as far as she was concerned, they might have been alone in a candlelit hacienda full of soft lights and low music.

'Enough,' he snapped. 'I don't do make-up.'

The other girls took the hint, backing away step by step in a timid, doe-eyed flock, dreaming wildly he might call one of them back.

'Go,' Xavier Martinez Bordiu insisted in a low, gravelly voice, flicking his wrist at the remaining girl. 'Go join your friends. You're not needed here.'

Abruptly, her eyes cleared and, as he watched them fill with tears of embarrassment, a pang of regret caught him unawares. Straightening up, he reached out to apologise, but she had already gone with the others and the double doors leading out of his apartment at the presidential palace had closed behind them.

What the hell was wrong with him?

As Xavier made a deep sound in his throat, feeling a stab of familiar pain, he saw the Floor Manager starting to panic. He made a signal to deflect the man's concern, but he was already calling. 'Water for Dr Martinez Bordiu.'

5

Xavier sat back again, oblivious to the splendour of his surroundings: chandeliers the size of houses, ivory fretwork screens, precious paintings banked up side by side as far as the eye could see on towering walls decked out in crimson silk.

This was a temporary stay at the President's personal invitation, but he had lived with such opulence all his life. It meant nothing to him. However sumptuous his living quarters, however attentive his staff, even a life of unremitting luxury could pall in the end. That was why he had trained to become a doctor. And that was partly the reason he had chosen to lose himself in Peru, in a medical project that meant everything to him.

His jaw clenched and then released again as he waited impatiently for the vanities of the woman who was shortly to interview him about the project to be indulged.

She had the dark flashing looks of a true South American beauty. She was voluptuous and provocative, with a fall of glossy, nut-brown hair cascading over her smooth tanned shoulders. And when she turned to look at him he saw the tip of her tongue creep out to moisten her lips.

He viewed her lazily through hooded eyes and saw her squirm a little on her seat to ease what he knew would be bolts of desire. He knew then he could have her after the show: here, where he was sitting, or straddling his lap on the hard, upright chair where she was having her make-up perfected...or there on the Aubusson rug in front of the wall of windows so that everyone in Lima could get an eyeful.

He had that effect on women. And somewhere along the way it had all become too easy for him.

He never got involved. He didn't need to. He didn't need anyone. He was fine by himself. He had trained himself to be that way. Loving and losing, they were the same thing as far as he was concerned—and better avoided.

But that didn't give him the right to trample rough-shod over other people's feelings, Xavier thought, mouthing a quick response as someone brought over a jug of iced water and a glass. His thought processes changed track suddenly. Shutting out the rest of the room, he ran over the moment he almost made someone cry—not in pictures, but emotions, and found he cared...he really cared.

He subdued the rush of relief that gave him as the presenter came to sit across from him on a matching sofa, and tuned his expression to neutral as the interview began.

CHAPTER ONE

'XAVIER MARTINEZ BORDIU! Are you sure, Henry?'

Shocked at hearing the name—even more shocked at blurting it out in a tone that made her boss's head shoot up—Dr Sophie Ford felt her cheeks flush red. She knew she only had herself to blame when Professor Henry Whitland levelled a thoughtful stare on her face.

'Xavier Martinez Bordiu is one of the finest physicians in Europe. We're lucky to have the chance to work with him,' he reproved her mildly. 'I can't think of anyone better to head up the immunisation programme in Peru.'

But Sophie wasn't listening. Images of piercing navy-blue eyes were flashing through her mind...and sun-streaked tawny-brown hair, the colour, lustrous and rich, like a glass of good brandy—

'Sophie... Sophie?'

While her head of department struggled to recapture her attention it took Sophie a few moments to shunt her thoughts back on track. 'I'm sorry, Henry. You were saying?'

He frowned. 'I've heard Dr Martinez is something of a maverick, leaving all that luxury behind him and those vast estates...half of Spain, wasn't it?' He shook his head and sighed as he thought of it. 'But he's bringing his Midas touch to medical projects now, so perhaps we should be grateful.'

He waited a moment, then stared at Sophie inquisitively. 'You're very quiet, Sophie. Is there anything else about him you think I should know?' Laying down his gold-rimmed spectacles, he pinched the bridge of his nose as he waited for her to answer.

Xavier Martinez Bordiu? Sophie played for more time with a dismissive gesture. Rumour said Xavier had become

Spain's most notable monument to chauvinism in a country hardly noted for the retiring nature of its men. Would she have volunteered for the project if she'd known who was in charge? Probably not.

'No, Henry,' she said, able to reassure him on one point at least. 'There are no skeletons in Dr Martinez Bordiu's closet as far as I am aware.' But even that wasn't strictly true, Sophie realised as her face burned a little hotter. 'I hear on the grapevine that he's become a great doctor,' she said, struggling to return to safer ground as her throat dried.

'You speak as if you already know him.'

'I used to,' Sophie admitted. 'I knew the Martinez Bordiu family when I was a child.'

'Ah,' Henry said.

Why did she have a sinking feeling he wasn't about to let the matter rest? Henry wanted to be a lot more than her boss at St Agnetha's, and it was fair to say a kind of understanding had developed between them. Henry lived in the same village as her mother, whose knowledge of him was minimal, but enough for her to describe him optimistically as a safe pair of hands. Sophie had no argument with that. Henry Whitland was kind, thoughtful and very well respected in his chosen field. And one day she would have to make a decision about her personal life…

'And Xavier?' he pressed.

Xavier, Sophie mused. The last time she'd seen him she'd been a hormonal teenager—but now she was a career woman with better things to think about than romance, she warned herself sternly.

'Xavier Martinez Bordiu,' Henry said again, with a touch more impatience.

'Yes?' Sophie said helpfully.

'Forgive my interest, but I can't help noticing how the mere mention of his name makes your face flush. I realise it's none of my business—'

'I should have known who was leading the team,' Sophie said with a shrug.

'Martinez Bordiu kept his name out of it until recently. You could hardly be expected to know. Does it make a difference to your application?'

'Do you mean, am I going to back out? No,' Sophie said firmly. Whatever problems might be associated with working for Xavier, she could handle them. Glancing at her watch, Sophie suddenly found herself longing to escape to the purposeful bustle of the wards.

'Must you dash off?' Henry said with a touch of petulance as she stood up to leave. 'I thought we could talk some more.'

'I should be getting back—'

'I do remember your connection with Martinez Bordiu now.'

Sophie tensed as she waited for him by the door.

'I remember some talk in the village of a terrible accident in Spain—and, forgive me, but am I right in thinking that your parents split up shortly after that—?'

'That's right,' Sophie confirmed abruptly. 'Now, if you don't mind, Henry—'

'Far be it for me to risk Sister Spencer's wrath,' he agreed. 'It's almost time for rounds. I'll walk with you.'

As they parted at the double swing doors that led into the children's ward, he put his hand on the sleeve of Sophie's white coat, stopping her. 'I'm sure Dr Martinez Bordiu will be delighted to see you again.'

That tugged a smile from Sophie that didn't quite make it to her eyes. She doubted Xavier would see it that way. 'It's kind of you to say so, Henry,' she managed politely.

'I wondered if we might discuss some of the wider issues regarding your posting over dinner tonight?'·

Sophie's stomach clenched uncomfortably. 'I'm not sure, I—'

'Just a quick snack? At that brasserie you love down the road.'

'The one you hate?' Sophie shot him a wry grin as she shovelled her hands into her pockets.

'I don't hate it,' he argued mildly. 'The music's a little loud.'

'Eight o'clock, then,' she agreed with a quick smile. 'I'll meet you there.'

It wasn't that she didn't enjoy Henry's company, Sophie reasoned as she pushed the double doors that led through into the ward and hurried to join the small group of junior doctors milling around the nurses' station. She just needed more time to work out exactly what role he played in her life.

Casting a preoccupied glance out of the window of the light aircraft, Sophie tried telling herself that the arrangement she had made with Henry was fine. Before she left England he had insisted she have the antique ring she was now absent-mindedly twirling round her finger. Their understanding was open-ended—no pressure, no deadlines; it was more of a thinking space than an engagement. He offered friendship and security. And security, as her mother had pointed out pragmatically, was exactly the sort of thing a career woman like Sophie would come to want. Eventually.

'Mark my words, you will want to settle down one day...'

Settle, maybe, Sophie mused, remembering her mother's forceful lecture. But settle *down*? She wasn't so sure about that.

She didn't feel ready for suburbia just yet. Maybe she never would, she thought, peering out of the window again. There was still so much she wanted to see, so much to do first. But her sensible self demanded a hearing: Henry was a man in his mid-forties, with a wealth of experience behind him...*behind him* being the operative phrase as far as her mother was concerned. She had delicately pointed out that a man like Henry was less likely to *make demands* on Sophie.

Sophie's lips hardened as she remembered what had caused her mother's apprehension where men were concerned. Home was supposed to be a sanctuary, but it hadn't proved to be that for her mother. It hadn't been that for

Sophie either, though she didn't bear any physical scars. She had only cowered on the stairs as a child, listening to the violence that stemmed from her late father's drunken rages. It was a miracle her mother had survived at all, let alone gone on to live a full and happy life—and that was only thanks to the resilience of the female spirit.

Shifting in her seat, Sophie forced her mind to close down on that part of her life and concentrate on Henry instead. He had proved himself the perfect mentor, a loyal colleague and a true friend. And maybe, when she was ready, he would make the perfect husband. She reminded herself that the large cabochon amethyst was just a friendship ring...and that lots of successful marriages were founded on friendship; then, slipping it off her finger, she fastened it safely inside the top pocket of her jacket.

'Look out of the window.'

Evie, the pilot, broke into Sophie's thought processes, tipping the wings to give her a better view. 'We're just starting to fly over the Nazca Lines.'

'I had no idea they covered such a vast area,' Sophie said. Gigantic stylised figures, carved by an ancient people, reached across the arid umber plain below them for as far as she could see.

'Some of them are over three hundred metres across and, on that scale, only visible from the air,' Evie informed her, banking steeply. 'I'll spin you around to get a better look.'

She was serious, Sophie realised, bracing her feet against the floor as the small aircraft stood on its nose. Willing herself to stay calm, she managed to keep her stomach in place as they rotated through a full turn. But then, as curiosity got the better of her, she opened her eyes. She could make out a monkey, a fish, a spider and some sort of bird, as well as numerous geometric figures all painstakingly carved into the wide span of desolate earth, before the female equivalent of the Red Baron straightened out her plane and flew on.

'How on earth?'

'No one knows,' Evie said, anticipating the question.

'When? How? Why? It's a complete mystery. Even Xavier—'

'Xavier?' Sophie cut in, viewing her attractive companion with a keener eye.

'Xavier Martinez. Isn't that who you're going to be working with? There's not much else happening out here apart from his medical project. But if you don't know him yet,' she said, without giving Sophie a chance to butt in, 'you soon will. That's his truck down there. And this is as far as I go.'

Sophie instinctively braced her feet again as the small plane plummeted down on a trajectory that had the ground screaming up at a furious rate to meet them.

'Damn!' Evie exclaimed as she levelled out for landing. 'One of these days I'll get that monument to male chauvinism to jump out of the way—or maybe even notice me. But not today,' she fumed, ramming on the brakes after touchdown.

Making a tight turn, she accelerated down the narrow, bumpy airstrip to where Sophie could see a rangy figure, casually dressed, lounging back against the side of a dusty brown pick-up truck.

Extending her hand as they stopped, Evie said, 'I take it they've equipped you with a radio. If that sexist brute gets too much for you and you need an out, just call me, OK?'

'I can handle Xavier Martinez,' Sophie said confidently, returning the firm handshake. 'We've known each other for years.'

'You obviously haven't met him lately.'

'No,' Sophie admitted. After the rumours she'd heard she couldn't resist probing just a little. 'When I did know him he was quite a charmer...'

'Charmer?' Evie demanded incredulously. 'People change. I give you a week,' she added, drawing to a halt within spitting distance of Sophie's new boss.

And then the pilot's door flew open and Xavier was right there, ducking his head inside the confined space, baiting Evie with a dark, searing glance. The heat flew in from outside the aircraft, enveloping them in a warm cloud of faintly spicy air, and the temperature inside the small cabin went soaring up.

'Women drivers!' he challenged in a low, husky voice.

That voice... How could she have forgotten that voice? Sophie wondered, as vibrations rippled up and down her spine. That lust-inducing Latin growl of censure and testosterone that had every woman within earshot figuratively licking her lips...except this woman, Sophie asserted, feeling her defence shields snap into place.

'Is it my fault you like to litter up the place?' Evie retorted smartly. 'Now clear off my runway, Don Juan. The light's not going to hold up for much longer, and I need to get away.'

'What about your passenger?' he cut in, straightening up so that Sophie's view out of the door was suddenly obstructed by a spread of rock-hard chest, clothed in a rugged, chequered shirt open at the neck to reveal a scoop of black cotton.

'Dr Sophie Ford, safely delivered. Would you care to sign the manifest—'

'What the hell?' He ducked in again and peered across. 'Is this some sort of a joke?'

A giant hand seemed to seize hold of Xavier's guts and wrench them out where his back used to be. A red mist descended over his eyes as he tried to control the emotion clawing at his senses. It was so real, so tangible, he tried clearing it from his eyes with the knuckles of one hand. If there was anything on this earth he never wanted to see, or hear from, again, it was a member of the Ford family. Every one of the promises he had made to himself back in Lima to improve his manner evaporated as he stormed round the front of the aircraft.

His angry footsteps accelerated Sophie's efforts to release her seat belt.

'So, it is you,' he growled, flinging her door as wide as it would go.

'Xavier. You must have known,' Sophie insisted calmly,

gathering up her wits along with her gear. She had no intention of allowing herself to be drawn into a confrontation with the navy-blue lasers currently trained on her face. And just when had his hair darkened to sepia and mutated into aggressive spikes that emphasized his incredible bone structure, instead of conforming slavishly to the longer, sleeker style that started a whole new fashion amongst his wealthy set years back? Just when had cool become hot?

'How do you work that out?' he demanded curtly, stabbing into her memories.

'Henry wired ahead—'

'Henry—' Xavier's mimicry stopped just the polite side of parody '—hasn't a clue what's going on out here. He can't get hold of me by radio, fax, or pigeon post when I'm in the high country. He should know that by now. He should make it his business to know,' he added firmly, his voice rising when Sophie started to interrupt. 'He should also know I don't carry passengers.'

'Passengers! I'm here to do a job,' Sophie retorted firmly.

'Well, there aren't any cushy clinics out here for you to waft around.'

Sophie bit her tongue. She wouldn't take the bait and get into an argument with him. Five minutes into their meeting, she already knew the only way to work with Xavier would be to keep everything impersonal—emotion-free. Once aroused, he was just the type of full-blooded male who provoked emotions she chose not to examine too closely. But she could see why he would be shocked to see her. It made her go a little way to accepting his behaviour. If there had been time she would have warned him—given him time to prepare. It had to pain him to be confronted with a face from the past, and one from a family he had every reason to despise. But the Xavier she had known years back would never have behaved like this—and his assumption that she wouldn't be capable of pulling her weight was inexcusable.

As she went to climb out he slammed one hard, unyielding fist against the door, stopping her.

'Get out of my way!' Sophie warned, levelling a red-hot glare into his eyes as she heaved against the door.

Evie's low whistle forced a brief pause between them.

'I'd love to stick around to see how this thing works out between you two, but sadly—' she shot a glance through the windscreen '—the light's failing and time's pressing on. I gotta go.'

'Fine,' Sophie said pleasantly, dumping her rucksack on the ground. 'Thanks for the ride.'

'My pleasure.'

'Now just a minute,' Xavier insisted savagely. 'You aren't going anywhere, Sophie Ford. Get back in there.'

But Sophie had already slipped under his arm, picked up her rucksack, and was powering away from the aircraft as fast as she could.

'Good luck, Sophie!' Evie shouted, leaning out of the window, as she wheeled the plane round and lined up for take-off. 'Don't forget what I told you. I'm only a plane ride away.'

As the engine noise rose to a crescendo Sophie paused a moment, dropping her heavy rucksack to the ground to raise her hand. The propellers were whipping up a storm of fine dust particles from the hard-baked earth, forcing her to try and protect her eyes as she waved. 'Thanks, Evie,' she yelled at the top of her voice. 'I won't forget!'

'I suppose you think that's smart?'

'What? I… Thank you,' Sophie was forced to say with surprise, when instead of continuing to berate her, Xavier snatched up the rucksack she had been carrying.

At least he was still a gentleman, she thought, then let out a grunt as he swung it back on to her shoulders.

'It will be interesting to see how long you last,' he called back to her as he made for the truck.

'I might surprise you.'

'I doubt it!' Sophie Ford! Xavier cursed his luck. The pampered product of an overwrought mother and a father— He shook his head and made a sound of utter contempt.

'Well, thank you for that,' Sophie shouted after him, firming her lips.

'Don't thank me,' Xavier warned as they reached his truck. 'You'll be begging to be sent home within the week.'

'Not a chance,' Sophie muttered back, rubbing the last of the dust from her eyes.

Flinging open the passenger door, Xavier offered her his hand. She ignored it.

'Where I'm going is no place for you,' he rapped when they were both safely installed inside the cab.

Personal considerations aside, he needed strong, no-nonsense people for his project in Peru, not some dizzy blonde who looked as if she had never got her fingernails dirty in her life. Resting his hands on the steering wheel, he slanted another long look at her. 'And the pace of the project is too fast for a soft-bred city girl like you.'

'I'm here to stay, Xavier,' Sophie said in a quiet, steely voice. 'Get over it. According to your own promotional literature you need doctors. I'm a qualified doctor—*ergo*, you need me.'

Xavier's only response to that was a bark of derision.

Quite a welcome! Sophie thought, biting her tongue. Reminding herself Xavier was her boss, she stayed cool as she ran through every one of the reasons that had brought her to Peru. Leaving him out of the equation, she'd made the right decision. Putting him back in? If fate had conspired to put her in the passenger seat right now, she was going to make damn sure he treated her as an equal from here on in.

'The first flight I can get you out of here is next week—'

Sophie cut across him angrily. 'Let me remind you that I signed a contract.'

'So?' he challenged harshly. 'I'll buy you out of it.'

'There isn't enough money in this world to buy me, Xavier.' If he thought his immense wealth could put her off he was sadly mistaken, Sophie thought, seething with fury. She lost no time disillusioning him. 'I'm here to do a job.

And there is absolutely no possibility that I am simply going to turn tail and run back home on your say-so.'

'That's all I need,' he said with a rough sound of impatience. 'A headstrong woman.'

'Too much for you?' she suggested dryly.

There was a time when little Sophie Ford would never have dreamed of taking him on, Xavier reflected grimly. But there were benefits to be drawn from that. He didn't have to pussyfoot around for one thing. He could get rid of her the minute the first opportunity presented itself. Contenting himself with a sardonic half-smile, he said nothing more. But a muscle worked in his stubble-shaded jaw, suggesting he would like to say plenty. Turning the key in the ignition, he gunned an aggressively tuned engine into life.

Xavier had always liked to tune his own engines, so nothing much had changed there, Sophie thought, as he took off with a burst of speed that knocked her back in the seat. And yet, she realised, sneaking another glance at him, everything else had changed. What was one of the richest men in Spain doing in the wilds of Peru? What had transformed his life to the extent that he had retrained as a doctor whilst juggling the demands of the Martinez Bordiu birthright? Deep down, Sophie knew she didn't even have to ask herself that question—but he was looking at her again, his sharp, knowing glance hunting for cracks in the defences she had built around her thoughts—and there was a lot more hidden than she cared for him to see.

Quickly pinning a neutral expression to her face, Sophie turned her head to stare blindly out of the window, but not before the grim smile tugging at Xavier's lips had caught hold of her composure and tied it in knots. He was so male, so blatantly virile, and there was no escape from him in the confined space. Was this how he treated women now? A mental picture of him thrashing about like a wounded animal, seizing a mate for a few moments' comfort, and then casting them aside the moment emotions came into play, made her pulse quicken with apprehension.

Determinedly turning her thoughts back to work, Sophie frowned. Surely he didn't imagine she'd crumble on the sole basis it didn't suit him to have her in Peru?

Her only crime, as far as she knew, was that she came from his past. But the accident haunted her too; it always would. She felt his loss keenly as she glanced across at him, but Xavier's lips only hardened as he sensed her scrutiny. She would just have to accept that empathy wasn't enough. The fact she knew about the accident only made him doubly determined to get rid of her. As first meetings with your new boss went, Sophie mused wryly, this one was a classic!

'It's been a long time, Sophie. You're looking good.' He caught her off-guard. Straightening up, Sophie instinctively moistened her lips, and even brushed back an errant strand of hair from her face before the calculating and faintly amused look in Xavier's eyes warned he was playing a very masculine game. She certainly hadn't come all the way to Peru to provide some male predator with his daily diversion.

The truck's small cab was like a pressure cooker. It was bog-standard-basic, with no add-on luxuries such as air-conditioning. No luxuries, full stop, Sophie thought, glancing around. It was stifling with heat, and over-cooked opinions. Snatching up the topmost item on a pile stacked on the seat between them, she began fanning herself distractedly.

'That's my clean washing,' Xavier informed her as he retrieved the square of black cotton from her hands.

Boxers! Sophie saw as he shook them out with one hand and went on steering with the other.

'Fold them, and put them back,' he instructed, as if having her wave his pants in the air was an everyday occurrence.

'I...I don't—'

'Do it,' he said, increasing speed.

Save it! Sophie warned herself, knocking her temper back into touch as she replaced the offending article with as little fuss as possible. She had six months to tame this tiger. She could afford to yield on the first occasion.

CHAPTER TWO

SOPHIE sat staring ahead for what felt like hours on end, while the truck bumped and snarled its way across miles of featureless rust-coloured plain. But finally, when neck-ache began to beat at her brain, she was forced to give in. Easing her head from side to side, she stole a glance at her companion. His character had changed for the worse—that much she knew already. Now it was time to see whether the years really had been as kind to him as first impressions suggested...

'Seen enough, Sophie?'

Well, his senses were as keen as ever.

'Enough to see you haven't changed,' she lied with every appearance of calm. Inwardly she was as churned up as she could ever remember. It was one thing playing the ice-queen to Xavier's blatant virility, but he was sending her senses haywire! He always had been attractive. But now, with every vestige of civilised man stripped away, he was a lot more dangerous—a fact her body attested to as it responded urgently to him. In fact, there was a whole orchestra thrumming an insistent pulse where at best a mild pelvic clench would normally signal the presence of some attractive male.

'Is that good, or bad?' he said, eyes crinkling, lips turned down in wry enquiry.

Sophie felt her senses flare as she ran the inventory. Good—because she really liked his hair shorter, and the fact that it had darkened with age. It was as thick as ever with sideburns losing definition in the black stubble on his jaw... She stopped for a moment. For her, the stronger the attraction, the greater the fear; it was a potent combination, she realised, forcing herself to continue. Good—because his tanned face was just as strong and lean as she remembered it; the type that could almost have been described as stereotypical 'carved out of granite' had it not been for some really great additions. The mobile mouth for instance…and those clued-up, laughing eyes… She sucked in a guilty breath as he returned her stare full throttle.

'You haven't given me an answer yet,' he said, turning his attention back to the rutted road. 'Good. Or bad?'

His resonant voice was strumming her like a practised hand on a finely tuned instrument, the same harmonious chord running through her from the crown of her head to the tips of her toes…and all of that long before her mind had a chance to register the melting pot of confident Latin male and shrewd, irresistible humour he managed to shoe-horn into the one short question.

'It's good to see you again, Xavier,' Sophie admitted carefully, aware that her lips were actually trembling. And bad? The few moments Sophie gave herself to consider this slipped away too quickly. 'Bad, because you don't want me here—' She slammed her mouth shut without even bothering to try and dig herself out of the hole. Was that really the best she could come up with? It sounded like a suck-up! The kind of simpering, no-brain remark the person he seemed to think she had grown into might make. The look on his face only confirmed her worst fears.

'Too right I don't,' he said brusquely.

She should have known. And now she was angrier with herself than with him. Trust her to fall for the brief interlude when he almost made it to polite! She should have known he was only softening her up for the verbal kill. Turning her face away, Sophie stared numbly as the bleak terrain flashed past.

'So now I get the silent treatment?' Xavier said, flashing her a glance.

What was she doing here anyway? Sophie asked herself angrily. She could practice medicine equally well back home. Fate? She dismissed that out of hand. Henry? That was more likely. Wide-open spaces before the net of suburbia closed over her. Space from Henry—

'So, no husband yet?' Xavier demanded.

The patronising question stabbed into her reverie. 'Is this what I'm missing?' Sophie murmured tensely.

'Don't flatter yourself, sweetheart. I asked a simple question.'

'It's none of your business, Xavier,' she flashed back. 'And let's get something straight. I may work for you but my private life's just that—private. I'm here to stay. Get used to it.'

'You sleep in here,' Xavier told her as he shouldered open a creaking tin door. 'I leave for the high country tomorrow morning at dawn.'

As Sophie dumped her rucksack on the ground, Xavier looked round the sparsely furnished room, thumbs firmly planted in the belt-loops of his snug-fitting jeans, inviting her to change her mind and beg him to let her return to her safe, cosy bed back in the UK.

At least it was clean, Sophie thought—floor newly swept, windows bright in their frames of peeling, yellowing paint. Taking in the dilapidation as well as the lack of amenities, she just nodded her head. 'Fine. I'll be ready first thing tomorrow,' she agreed evenly.

Xavier shifted position, drawing himself up. Asserting his authority. Sophie felt herself instinctively bristling in response.

'I said *I'd* be heading for the high country. You'll be staying here.'

'Oh, really?' Sophie knew she was overtired. The last thing she wanted was a fight. But she had no intention of backing down either.

'Yes, really,' he stated firmly.

They were confronting each other tensely like two stalking tigers. Xavier broke the silence first, adding a little more chaos to his hair with an impatient pass of his strong, tanned fingers.

'Look, Sophie,' he said, applying a very masculine brand of reason. 'This place needs sorting out before morning. A pile of new medical supplies have arrived, and they all need putting away in some sort of order. Then the details need filing—'

'If you wanted a filing clerk you should have requested one in your list of job opportunities in the recruitment pack,' Sophie pointed out.

'We're a team. We share the work-load.'

'Then may I suggest you stay with me here at base until we have completed the office work and stock-take. Then we can both travel on to the high country together.'

There was just enough of a pause to show that she had got through to him.

'What I'm trying to say—'

'I think I know what you're trying to say, Xavier,' Sophie countered firmly.

As she watched his eyes narrow she felt a thread of apprehension run through her. Xavier had become a difficult, complex man, not someone it was sensible to range herself against. But teamwork meant sharing everything, didn't it? From clearing up, to treating patients. 'I'd better sort out my things…freshen up,' she said, taking a different tack in the hope of cooling things down.

'Of course.' He gave her a mock bow, but his disturbing gaze held her own until Sophie's desperately searching fingers managed to locate the fastenings on her bulging rucksack and she could pretend to busy herself with that. But before he left she wanted another answer. 'Who sleeps in here?' she said, surveying the row of camp beds.

'Me,' Xavier said with a shrug, 'and whoever else drops in.'

Taking a deep breath, Sophie swallowed back the panic that threatened to choke her. She was here to work. She had to forget every one of her personal concerns and just get on with it. 'How exhilarating,' she managed evenly. 'I shall never know what to expect from one night to the next.'

Xavier shot her a darkly amused stare. 'You won't be here that long,' he promised.

'Don't count on it,' Sophie murmured under her breath, glancing around.

'My apologies,' Xavier said as he watched her. 'I don't know what you were expecting, but this isn't the Ritz. It's just an old place I'm using until I get something else built.'

'I think it's all quite satisfactory, thank you,' Sophie countered. 'Apart from having to share with you, it's exactly what I expected.' She saw his lips kick up at one corner, and his eyes begin to gleam. 'Bathroom?' she demanded briskly, though her heart was still juddering.

'Bathroom?' The drawled exclamation was accompanied by another humour-laced stare. 'Turn right outside the door, third bush down—'

'OK, Xavier,' Sophie said calmly. 'I can see I'm not getting anywhere with you being polite. So, let's both shoot from the hip. Don't waste your breath. You don't frighten me.' But the feelings he awoke in her did, Sophie acknowledged, struggling to ignore them.

'Good,' he said mildly, throwing up his hands in mock-surrender.

'So when do I get to meet the rest of the team?' she said, adopting her professional manner.

'Impatient, Sophie?'

'Keen to get on with the job.' And to be too busy to think about anything else.

'The rest of the team are in place now,' he said. 'I've been flying backwards and forwards from Spain for some time now. All that's left is for me to finish my tour here and check that everyone has everything they need.'

'And I fit in, where?'

Xavier's eyes hardened thoughtfully as he looked at her. If he had seen her name before she arrived she wouldn't even have got this far. And he wasn't about to tell her that the last position on his list, the position she thought she was filling, was for his second in command—a doctor who would accompany him wherever he went. 'Are you hungry?'

Sophie locked eyes. 'You didn't answer my question yet.'

'And you didn't answer mine,' he said easily.

They stood confronting each other in silence for a few moments until Sophie saw something change in his eyes, then she quickly looked away.

'We'll discuss your position over dinner,' he said. But the curl of his mouth, the look in his eyes, suggested, *missionary*, or *dominant*?

Defences formed in her mind and sprang to her lips. 'I don't know what kind of arrangement you have with your other female colleagues,' Sophie said coldly, 'but let's get this straight from the outset, Xavier, I *never* mix business with pleasure. And I don't find you the least bit attractive,' she blurted when she saw the amusement behind his eyes.

'You are hungry,' he murmured confidently.

As a flood of feelings she had kept at bay for a lifetime threatened to overwhelm her, Sophie reminded herself forcefully how much she wanted this job. 'As it happens, you're right. I am hungry,' she said, relieved she could sound so cool.

'So, why don't you leave the unpacking for now?'

Sophie relaxed fractionally.

'By the way, where *do* you want to sleep?' He echoed her glance down the line.

'Next to the window?' Sophie suggested. The first three bunks were already occupied—one of them by him, presumably. A two-bunk gap was the best she could hope for, so she'd take it.

Picking up her rucksack, Xavier dumped it on top of the last bunk. 'After you,' he said, gesturing towards the open door.

If possible, the kitchen was even more basic than the sleeping quarters. An ancient stove fed by bottled gas, and blackened with use, sat squat in one corner. A single cold tap dripped rhythmically over a large, rectangular pot sink crazed with age, and above that some hastily erected shelves were haphazardly stacked with assorted tinned food of uncertain origin.

'I can feel your concern coming right at me through my shirt,' Xavier observed, sounding pleased. 'Time to book that plane ticket home?'

'No,' Sophie said flatly. And, as long as it was only concern she could sense, that was fine by her.

'Well, it's clean,' he said, glancing around with relish. 'At least I can reassure you on that point.'

Reaching up to the top shelf, he brought down a crude wooden box. 'I've got some fresh supplies,' he explained, tipping it a little so that Sophie could see inside. 'The local big shot gets me anything I need. He offered me his youngest daughter yesterday.'

'Did you accept?' For some reason his gag bothered her more than it should have done, Sophie realised, wishing she could call back the question.

'Joke?'

'Ha ha,' she intoned dutifully, keeping her face in neutral while a rogue shaft of sensation warned her not to think about Xavier in any way at all, other than as her boss.

'So,' she continued a little too brightly. 'What do we have here?' As his attention returned to their food supplies, Sophie's gaze was drawn to his powerful arms. On one wrist he wore a black leather wristband, which had been his younger brother Armando's, and on the other, a no-nonsense steel watch.

The sight of the wristband forced Sophie's thoughts into a dark, shadowy corner. No wonder Xavier had been shocked to see her. How could he talk about the past without making some reference to the accident? He had to log everything as *before* or *after*. People who came *after* were safe, because they didn't know, didn't have to know. She was very much *before* the accident. She must have been the last person on earth he wanted around, she reasoned, telling herself to go easy on him.

Xavier stopped rooting through the food and stared back at her. Instinctively, he glanced at the wristband and, just for an instant, Sophie saw the pain was still as raw, still as devastating and undiminished as on the day Armando had been killed. Surely he couldn't still be blaming himself? In that moment she longed to reach out to him, to touch him in some way, but the closed expression on his face warned her not to try.

'The food's pretty good,' he said, confirming her suspicions, as he turned back to the prospect of supper with a force that suggested he was keen for them both to leave the past undisturbed. Plunging his hand into the depths of the box, he murmured, 'Now this looks like *Pachamana*.' Lifting out an earthenware pot, he held it up.

'Which is?'

'Various meats, and vegetables.'

'Meats?'

'Still a vegetarian?' he guessed.

'Sorry.'

'Don't apologise for that.'

He made it sound as if she had plenty to be sorry about without the fact that she was a vegetarian, Sophie thought wryly. 'Do you have anything else?'

Xavier shot her a look that suggested this foray into domesticity was about as far from fun for him as it got. Remembering she had vowed to be nice to him, Sophie said, 'Don't you miss that wonderful chef your mother used to employ at Casa Bordiu?'

'I don't miss anything about my old life—with the exception of seeing my parents most days,' he said, the expression in his eyes hidden from her as he turned away.

'But all that opulence and then this—' Instantly, Sophie knew she had gone too far, delved too deeply into realms he would rather forget. When he turned around the shadows in his eyes were darker.

'Opulence?' He spat out the word like poison, and then drew himself up to lash her with his pain. 'Have you forgotten how my brother was killed? Opulence—' He stopped, his face an ugly mask, but the words dredged up from some fetid place at his core hung in the air between them like a dissonant chord.

'I hadn't forgotten,' Sophie said gently.

'Don't bring it up again,' he rapped, each word staccato.

But she hadn't, he had, Sophie registered.

Xavier turned angrily on himself. This was his worst nightmare come true. All he could see when he looked at Sophie was her father. She had the same blue eyes, the same blonde hair, and the same slim build. On her father it had been an insipid combination—perfectly suited to his character. Xavier's lips curled in self-disgust. It was no use trying to shovel blame for the accident on to that weak excuse for a man. The blame for Armando's death rested squarely on his own shoulders—one day he'd have to confront that, but not today—and not with Sophie Ford. He cast another glance at her. She was her father's daughter all right. She looked so like him. She shared the same tainted blood. Women like her were good for one thing only...

His senses flared as he looked at her. With that in mind he would have to build a few bridges. Didn't they say revenge was a dish best served cold? Though when they got between the sheets, he'd take his hot. Little Sophie Ford had ripened like a peach for the plucking—and he was developing quite an appetite.

'It's baked over a heated stone inside a hole in the ground,' he said pleasantly.

Sophie actually flinched as she hurried to pay attention. It was as if the tense exchange had never taken place. Xavier might have been conducting a presentation to a class of students, she realised, as he carried on describing the food they had available.

'What else have you got?' she said, glad to play along.

'*Papa a la Huancaina*,' he said, removing a lid from the second pot with a flourish.

She was relieved to see him relaxing a little. She guessed his emotions had stalled ten years back at the time of the accident. Rather than confront the deep well of grief inside him at the time, he had simply shut himself off from it. This wasn't the Xavier she knew—this was a man who cared for nothing and no one; a man who had forgotten how to love, Sophie mused, vowing to cut him some slack.

'It could have been prepared especially for you, *señorita*: boiled potatoes with cheese bathed in a mild chilli sauce.'

At least he had forgotten to scowl this time, Sophie noticed wryly. Maybe there was hope for a reasonable working relationship after all. 'Sounds great,' she agreed.

'And for pudding we have tropical fruit.' He introduced each one in turn. 'Papaya, mango, passion fruit.'

'So, what did you have to give the local big shot in exchange for all this?' she teased. But from the minutest change in his eyes she saw that her attempt at humour had missed its mark by a mile.

'Is that important?'

His voice was soft and unthreatening, but Sophie knew she had touched a nerve. There was something in his eyes— unanswered questions that must have lain dormant in his mind for years. Suddenly something occurred to her: surely he didn't imagine she was one of the people who thought him responsible for his brother's death? The very idea was offensive to her, ludicrous.

'If it was anything to do with the full moon and virgins, no, not particularly,' she said in a desperate attempt to lighten the situation. She leapt with alarm as the box hit the floor with a slap.

'Is that what you think of me?' Xavier demanded quietly. Tension swirled around them like a mist, making the tiny kitchen feel a good deal smaller.

'Of course not.' Sophie was frightened by the intensity in

his gaze, and at the same time the thought of Xavier doing anything underhand was inconceivable.

Silently, he returned to the business of lighting the cooker, signalling the end of the exchange.

They had to get to know each other all over again, Sophie realised, as she watched him. The impetuous teenager she had once been was as far removed from her present incarnation as Xavier was from the life-loving young aristocrat who used to rip up the roads with his high performance cars.

Over supper they discussed nothing more controversial than the various treatments for asthma, a condition Sophie had suffered from since infancy. Then, after helping him to clear up the dishes, she made an excuse to escape to her own bed. Away from Xavier's distracting presence, Sophie hoped it might be possible to get her thoughts in order and have a decent night's sleep before their early start the next morning.

Snuggling deep into her sleeping bag, half-clothed, she meant to spend an hour or so quietly mulling over everything that had happened. But the moment her head touched the pillow her eyes drifted shut, and she knew nothing more until an insistent tapping on the window brought her fully awake the next morning.

Gathering her thoughts, Sophie clambered out of the low-slung bed and stared out of the window. A Peruvian couple stood waiting outside, a broad smile on the woman's round face, with just a little more tension showing on the face of her male companion.

'Just a minute,' Sophie called to them as a cluster of impressions struck her all at once: Xavier's bed hadn't been slept in, the floor felt chilly under her bare feet, even though the sun was beaming promisingly outside, she was in Peru! Excitement ripped through her as she pulled on her jeans and made for the door. Whoever the couple were, they looked friendly, and Xavier had to be somewhere around…didn't he?

She was here to do a job, Sophie warned herself as she went to open the outer door to the clinic. Even if an unashamedly primitive part of her insisted on responding to the fact that Xavier was masculinity incarnate—a fact that excited and worried her in equal measure—it was high time she got on with it.

But where were the keys? And, more importantly, where was Xavier?

She was fully awake now, her senses on full alert, and she had the unmistakable impression that she was alone. Swinging around, she scanned the sparsely furnished room, and there, on top of the table where they had eaten supper the previous evening, she saw a large bunch of keys resting on top of a sheet of paper. Snatching up both the keys and the paper, she made for the door, reading as she went.

Juan and Lola will take good care of you—

The hand holding the sheet of A4 clenched automatically, scrunching the rest of Xavier's message into indecipherable gibberish.

He'd gone without her!

CHAPTER THREE

SOPHIE made a furious sound as she wrestled with the door locks. How could she have been so complacent? If Xavier thought she had come all the way to Peru to be incarcerated at Base Camp like some undependable youth— And she didn't need *looking after*!

Swinging open the door, the sunlight hit her face. It was gloriously warm and, as the woman waiting outside began to speak, Sophie's anger took a back seat.

'Welcome to Peru, Dr Ford!'

A genuine beam of delight split the older woman's face from ear to ear, displaying an enviable set of strong white teeth. 'I'm Lola,' she said, cocking her head to one side. Then she sighed wearily as she turned to view the man hovering in her substantial shadow. 'And this is my husband, Juan.'

'You speak English,' Sophie said with relief, returning the smile as she extended her hand. 'As you guessed, I'm Sophie Ford, a new doctor with the project. I'm very pleased to meet you, Lola. And I'm relieved to—'

'Not as relieved as I am to have another woman around the place,' Lola interrupted, bustling past her into the clinic. 'Take the bike,' she instructed Juan. 'Put it away. Mind you stand it up properly.'

Sophie smiled. Something told her this wasn't the first time Juan had received his orders for the day from Lola. 'Bike?' she said ingenuously, following Lola into the clinic, the kernel of an idea beginning to take shape in her mind.

'*Sí*,' Lola said, moving behind the improvised counter to check the boxes Xavier had found time to bring in from the truck before he left.

Sophie tried again. 'You arrived here on a bike?' The image of Lola and Juan teetering along together on a pushbike seemed unlikely, particularly as Xavier had said the next village was quite a distance away.

'*Sí,*' Lola said with a heavy sigh. 'This man of mine is a little crazy,' she confided fondly, twirling a finger around her head to illustrate the point. 'He thinks he is a Hell's Angel.'

'Ah, a motorbike.' A motorbike! Sophie could hardly contain her excitement. Her idea was rapidly blossoming into a fully fledged plan. 'Could I borrow it?'

'Borrow it! For what? Where would you go?' Lola declaimed, her eyes as large as saucers. 'No, Dr Ford,' she said firmly. 'This is not your London with traffic lights and zebras crossing. This is Peru, with spectacled bears and monkeys!'

'Wonderful!' Sophie said as her mind took a flight over the rugged terrain. She hadn't even known there were bears in Peru. Well, except for Paddington, of course, who, according to the luggage tag thoughtfully placed around his neck by Michael Bond, the author of his bear-tales, came from Darkest Peru.

Gradually Sophie became aware of Lola's curious glances and realised what a great first impression she was giving—a daydreaming doctor with hair sticking out all over her head, bare feet, and a rumpled top she'd slept in—hardly an image to inspire confidence in the patients. 'What I mean is,' she tried again, running her fingers through her hair in a failed attempt to tame it, 'would you let Juan take me to find Xavier? You see,' she said, uncomfortable with the lie, but forced to go on with it, 'I overslept this morning, and he had to leave without me…'

Maybe it was the sheer desperation in her voice that had persuaded Lola to loan out her husband for the day, Sophie decided, clinging to Juan's scrawny form as he leaned low over the handlebars. Right now, Sophie wished she hadn't! The bike's bald tyres kept skimming the edge of the narrow track, and beyond that there was a sheer drop half hidden in cloud. There was no point trying to say anything to Juan. He couldn't hear a thing with the wind whistling in his ears. All Sophie could do was close her eyes.

She felt the ground smooth out abruptly and then her eyes flew open in alarm as Juan executed a wide, skidding turn. The first thing Sophie knew of the fall was staring at the dusty ground, wondering how she got there. The next few impressions came in a rush all at once. Xavier's feet by her face, his voice like a report from a gun: '*Estúpida!*' Shock that stopped her breathing for a few moments… And pain—in her leg, in her head, on her hands—everywhere. She shook him off furiously when he went to haul her to her feet.

'What are you doing here, Xavier?' Sophie struggled to recapture what little remained of her dignity, swiping dust from her face, mouth and hands while she waited for his explanation.

'I heard the bike,' he growled in a menacing tone, putting his face very close up to hers. 'Sound travels in the mountains.'

He went to check her over, but Sophie broke away. 'So, where the hell am I?' she said, looking around. The groomed track where she was standing and the impressive gates in front of her might have been constructed to harmonise with nature but they smacked of high-spending tourists, not local patients.

Ignoring her question for the moment, Xavier turned to Juan. 'Why have you brought Dr Ford here?'

'I'm sorry. Dr Ford insisted—'

'Never mind,' Xavier said, resting his hand on Juan's shoulder. 'Go and get yourself something to eat and drink before you start back.' He turned back to Sophie and looked her up and down. 'Are you all right?' he demanded sharply. His glance took in the bloodstains on the leg of her jeans.

'Where is this?' Sophie demanded tensely, ignoring his question. 'Well? Are you going to tell me, or shall I just go and find out for myself?' She tipped her chin in the direction Juan had taken. 'I take it this road leads somewhere? Somewhere grand?' she suggested acerbically.

'Does your leg hurt?' Xavier persisted, seeing her wince as she put her weight on it.

'Don't change the subject,' Sophie warned. 'Well, Xavier, are you going to answer me or not?'

He backed up a few steps and shot a glance at the sign she now saw was discreetly concealed in some shrubbery. 'This is the Rancho del Condor, a luxury lodge and spa,' he said evenly, 'and you look like you could use a bath.'

Sophie's lips compressed in an angry line. 'The Rancho del Condor!'

'Come,' he said, waving her forward. 'Now that you're here I'd better take a look at that leg.'

'I can deal with it myself, thank you. I take it there's antiseptic at the Rancho—' Abruptly her voice faltered and she swayed towards him. Shock, Sophie realised hazily, hands flailing desperately as she grabbed on to the only thing that was stable within her reach—Xavier.

'What am I going to do with you?' he demanded sharply. What indeed? he mused, supporting her around the waist. But then he was forced to reel in his baser instincts. He could feel her trembling. She was badly shaken up. Maybe she had concussion. He'd have to check her over thoroughly. 'You could have been killed,' he pointed out, stabbing a look at her. 'And then—'

'And then what? You'd care?' Sophie demanded, angry with herself, with Xavier, with everything.

'And then I'd be short of one doctor,' he countered smoothly.

By the time they made it round the corner and the full splendour of her new surroundings was revealed, Sophie had recovered sufficiently to shake herself free. 'Oh, I see!' She narrowed her eyes, taking it all in. The immaculately groomed site was cosily sandwiched between towering rock faces, which provided the topographic equivalent of a heat-retaining soup bowl. But it was the buildings that really captured her attention. An indolent sprawl of tented pavilions, or wood-framed villas, she saw on closer inspection, draped with some flowing material to give them the appearance of rather glamorous rustic dwellings. But there was nothing remotely rustic about the Rancho del Condor, she realised tensely as Xavier stopped outside an open-fronted reception area.

'Dr Martinez Bordiu—can I be of some further service to you?'

Sophie's mouth tightened a fraction more as Xavier stopped to speak to the beautiful young Peruvian girl, wearing a pared down version of her national costume.

'Well, Sophie?' Xavier said, turning to her finally, 'do you want that bath, or not?'

'I'd sooner eat my own feet! Is this your idea of a joke?'

'A joke?' he said mildly.

Moving out of earshot of the girl, Sophie drew Xavier with her. 'So this is where you stay,' she said, glancing around. 'Nice place you've got here, Doctor.'

'What are you getting at?' Xavier demanded, dipping his head to catch her high-octane whisper.

'I'm accusing you of double standards,' Sophie said flatly. 'One for you, another for the rest of us.'

'What are you talking about?'

'Just this…' Sophie said, her expression hardening as she gestured around. 'Rancho del Condor.'

'Now just a minute—'

'Don't you just a minute me,' she warned, snatching her arm out of his grasp.

But stamping down on her damaged leg at the same time made her wince. The graze she guessed was hiding under her jeans was really starting to sting and, to her horror, she felt tears burning her eyes—tears she had no intention of allowing Xavier to see. Keeping her head down, she gingerly tested her weight first on one foot and then the other. No serious harm done, she realised thankfully. Surface abrasions caused by the rasp of fabric on her skin must have caused the damage.

'Let me see your leg—'

'No.' She stumbled back and away from him. Suddenly her arms were bound very tightly to her sides, and then she was swung off her feet completely and settled into his arms.

'I'm getting you inside before you get yourself into any more trouble,' Xavier said flatly. 'You need cleaning up— and a bath.'

Sophie could hardly breathe through the panic that swept over her the moment she felt his arms close around her. 'Let me go. Let me go, please.'

'That leg needs cleaning up,' Xavier said firmly, increasing his grip as she struggled to get away, 'and a sick doctor is the last thing I need.'

'No, you don't understand. I can't—'

'Can't what?' he exclaimed impatiently, heading deeper into the exclusive resort.

Her heart was pumping so fast now Sophie only managed to gasp out, 'I'm sorry—'

'Sorry!' Xavier exclaimed, settling her more comfortably in his arms. 'I'm the one who's sorry. I ask for a doctor, and they send me a mad woman who chooses to ride pillion behind the speed freak of the Andes.'

She was glad he couldn't see her face—couldn't see the stricken look she knew was painted across it. The look that came from fear...fear of ceding control to a man, any man, and Xavier most of all. Right now he might have emerged from the darkest corner of her blackest nightmare, and all because he was a full-blooded male with all the needs and desires that went with the territory—*sex, force, violence*—the mantra played over and over in her head, keeping rhythm with his strides, until she thought she would go quite mad. She wasn't just frightened, Sophie realised, she was terrified. 'Put me down, please,' she begged hoarsely. 'I think I'm going to be sick.'

'Aren't you being a little melodramatic?' Xavier said evenly without breaking stride. 'I am a doctor. A little puke doesn't worry me.'

'I mean it.'

'Look, we're here,' he said, stopping outside one of the largest luxury villas. 'You can walk by yourself now.' He set her down and stood back. 'The bathroom's just inside—go and be sick in there if you think you need to.'

The moment she was free again Sophie felt the panic subside. She took a few deep breaths to be certain. 'I feel a lot better, thank you.'

'In,' Xavier said impatiently, flinging open the door.

'Which charm school did you go to?' Sophie demanded as she turned to confront him.

'The same one as you, I imagine.'

Her whole body was on fire where he'd held her, Sophie realised, as she stepped into the villa. But it was a beguiling heat, not the dangerous flame of drunken passion that brought nothing but pain in its wake. Touch was as unique to the individual as a fingerprint.

'What do you think?' Xavier demanded, breaking into her thoughts.

He was waiting for her verdict on the accommodation, Sophie realised. 'Very nice.' She gazed round the extravagantly furnished room. It combined the best of modern technology as far as sound and vision was concerned with some fabulous examples of the local crafts—wood carving, ceramics and colourful textiles all shown off to best advantage by flickering candles and carefully positioned lighting.

'I'm glad you like it,'

'Oh, I really do,' Sophie said, her voice crackling with tension as she drew a few fast conclusions. 'The rest of the team gets to stay at base camp with a cold-water shower and a beat-up kitchen, while you stay here in the lap of luxury having a good laugh at our expense.'

'The water would have heated up if you'd been patient—'

Sophie cut him off with a glare. 'I don't imagine patience comes into it here at the Rancho del Condor,' she said, taking her time to turn a slow circle, eyebrows raised at an expressive angle.

'Maybe not,' Xavier conceded, 'but this is not my—'

'Not your what, Xavier?' Sophie demanded. 'Not your idea of something to share with the rest of us?'

Strolling around the room, she began to tick off in a highly charged voice, 'Huge and undoubtedly very comfortable teak bed with…oh yes, unbleached linen sheets. A plump duvet loaded with hand-embroidered cushions. *Two* sofas…a collection of magazines and books…*air conditioning*?' She threw him a look full of accusation. 'And what's this…don't tell me—'

Xavier followed her through an impressive archway, hand-carved in wood, into another large room.

Standing on the threshold, Sophie planted her hands on her hips and looked around. 'The bathroom you mentioned—all clad in marble, and a Jacuzzi made for two.'

'Shall we try it out?'

There was laughter in Xavier's eyes, Sophie noticed, and something else. Strange forces were beginning to invade her senses, and before she could turn away from him they turned her limbs soft and compliant where only moments ago she had been stiff with defiance. She tried putting Xavier out of her mind, but the light was hazy gold filtered through muslin at the windows, and the temperature was body warm. There was a beguiling aroma, as if someone had been in just before them to spritz some rare and exotic scent into the air. She had never seen such a selection of full-sized bath oils and lotions in her life, and though she recognised most of the exclusive names the temptation to open just one or two was overwhelming. She felt like a child let loose in a sweet shop…except the sweetness here offered a different kind of stimulation, and she felt her nipples tightening in response as she paused and cast another look at Xavier. Rancho del Condor was a place out of time, a magical, mystical place and, for a few rare moments, even the fear of raw masculinity she had lived with all her life seemed to recede. Surely she hadn't come to such a dramatic and beautiful land as Peru to endure the same hang-ups she lived with back home?

Sophie cast a languorous stare through the voile-draped

window at the vista of rock face and foliage that lay beyond the luxury villa. She was alone with Xavier in a romantic setting she had never expected to encounter in Peru, let alone with him. It was an opportunity that might never come again—but there was his pride to contend with; she had pushed him away, acted like an ice-queen. But that didn't make the compulsion to feel his strength beneath her hands go away.

Sophie gazed up. She was close enough to inhale Xavier's warm, spicy scent—close enough to touch him, to hold him. She was bathed in his aura, intoxicated by her surroundings, and emotions that had been suppressed too long made her reckless. Reaching out, she rested her hands either side of his waist, fingers splaying down to embrace the strength in his hips.

Xavier jerked back, leaving her dazed for a moment.

'What are you doing?' His eyes narrowed. This wasn't how he planned it. She got it on his terms, or not at all. He gave the stark outline of her erect nipples a frank appraisal. She had great breasts, full and tip-tilted. He could imagine her naked without any trouble—fine-boned frame, long, slender legs to wrap around his waist, and those full lips parted just like they were now, but noisily sucking in plumes of air when he finally gave her what she was begging for. He had seen that look on women's faces countless times before. It had ceased to stir him way back, but the sight of Sophie Ford in an erotic frenzy pleased him greatly. It made him more determined than ever to keep her waiting. By punishing the daughter he could already feel some small relief, as if he was reaching down into hell and punishing her father as well.

He saw her eyes clear. She seemed lost, dazed. If he hadn't known her father he might have been fooled at that moment into thinking she had suddenly come to her senses. But hadn't he seen that look somewhere before—that mock-penitent I'm-as-innocent-as-the-day-is-long look? It was exactly the same expression her father had worn right after the accident! Did she think she could play him like a pike on a line? No problem, Dr Ford, Xavier mused sardonically. If that's where you're coming from, I'll give you all the sex you want—but at a time of my own choosing, not yours.

'I need to check you out for signs of concussion, and take a look at that leg,' he said, a pleasant and professional tone masking the true line of his thoughts. 'There should be a first aid kit in this cupboard.'

Shock at what she had done—at Xavier's reaction to it— filled Sophie with successive waves of fury and shame. 'You seem to know this place well,' she said angrily, defensively.

'I should do,' Xavier said cuttingly, removing what he needed from a square white box. 'It belongs to my mother.'

Sophie's face reddened as she realised her mistake.

'I come here on a regular basis to check on things for her. Check the KPIs against the targets and budgets I've agreed with the local management—'

'KPIs?' Sophie seized the chance to return to safer ground.

'Key performance indicators—companies have vital signs just like the body,' Xavier said, glancing up. 'It's how I measure all my business activities, and my staff's performance—'

'Even mine?' she cut in, then immediately wished she hadn't.

'I haven't got round to you yet. But I will,' he promised. 'Now, take your jeans off.'

Sophie's mouth dried. 'I'll roll them back.'

With a fast, impatient glance, Xavier caught hold of her calf. 'Will you relax while I clean this leg?' he demanded as she tensed.

Sophie complied, bracing herself against his touch as much as the antiseptic. 'How long will you stay here?' she said to distract herself.

'I'd no intention of staying here at all until you turned up. I only broke my journey to collect the data I mentioned. This project is as important in its way as the medical programme. It brings much-needed work to the area.'

'Your mother's idea?'

'Rancho del Condor was my gift to her. She needed something after—' He stopped as if he had said too much. A flare of anger touched his face, and he let go of her leg as if suddenly he couldn't bear to touch her. Then, gathering himself, he continued treating her again as if nothing untoward had occurred.

He had supported his mother to take her mind off the tragic death of Armando, her younger son, to bring a sense of purpose back into her life. Sophie couldn't help but feel a little warmer towards him. He was a difficult man, but he still cared.

'I have always handled the business end for her,' Xavier said, cutting into her musings. 'But without my mother's flair…' He shrugged expressively as he looked up. Briefly their eyes locked, and then he looked away.

She should have known, Sophie thought. Everything about the exclusive establishment bore the unmistakable stamp of Xavier's glamorous Italian mother. She could only guess at the emotional wounds that the woman must have sustained following the tragic death of Xavier's brother. Now there was someone who must truly hate her family and everyone connected with it, she realised, suppressing a shudder.

'Am I hurting you?' Xavier asked, misreading the movement beneath his hands.

'No, not at all,' Sophie said. 'You were telling me about your mother,' she prompted, hungry to hear more.

'She stayed at a few luxury lodges in Africa, and persuaded me that something similar could be achieved here—a retreat from the stresses of the city where the comfort of the guests doesn't come at the expense of the environment. You're fine,' he said, reverting to doctor-speak again. 'You're shaken up, a few scratches; you've been lucky.'

'Thank you, Doctor.'

'Don't mention it.'

For a brief moment, as he straightened up, they almost smiled at each other, and then, as if remembering the roles the past had imposed upon them, they became guarded again.

'Perhaps I should take you back to base. It would be simpler—'

'For you, or for me?' Sophie broke in. 'I've no intention of being stuck on the sidelines, Xavier, while you do all the things I read about in my joining details.' As his eyes flared a warning, Sophie seized the challenge. 'I may work for you, but please remember I signed a contract based on your promotional material. Are you telling me now that I was misled?'

Xavier stared at her. 'Why, Sophie? Are you thinking of suing me?'

'I'm not joking, Xavier.'

'We'll talk about this in the morning,' he said, moving back through the arch into the bedroom. 'It was a very long journey. You should find everything you need,' he added, as if suddenly he couldn't wait to get away.

'Like last time? I wake up and find you gone?'

Now he did smile—a slow, brooding, dangerous smile that sent a shiver racing down the length of her spine.

'There is a solution,' he observed in his low, husky voice.

'Oh, really? And what's that?'

'I stay here,' he said easily. 'That way you can keep an eye on me.'

'In here?' Sophie demanded. 'With me?'

'It is a very big bed.' Xavier's lips curved in a smile as he contemplated working off his contempt for her family in such pleasurable circumstances.

'No way!'

Staring at her tense, angry face, he remembered her coming on to him just a short while back. He'd make her pay for the games she liked to play, and pay and pay again, until she was so desperate she got down on her knees and begged him for it...

'But if you're going to abandon me anywhere...'

When he saw the change in her face Xavier had to admit he was impressed. Tease, to ice-queen, and then on to insolent defiance in no time flat.

'If this is the accommodation that comes with the job, it will do.' Sophie shrugged expressively.

'*Touché*—for now, Dr Ford,' Xavier conceded, shooting her a brooding glance. 'I'll be right next door,' he promised, turning on his heel. 'Just call me if you need anything. Meanwhile, why don't you make the most of that Jacuzzi, and then get changed while I order dinner?' He turned, pausing with his hand on the door as he looked at her. 'It will give me a chance to brief you on our work out here while we eat.' And the rest, he mused, as some very primitive urges took him over.

'I'm afraid you'll have to take me as I am.'

'My pleasure.'

'I don't have anything clean to wear,' Sophie explained, viewing her bloodstained jeans. It was a relief to have something else to stare at apart from Xavier's dark eyes.

He could find no way past her defences. 'That isn't a problem. You know my mother,' he added when Sophie looked at him blankly. 'She insisted there should be a boutique here. Go,' he said, gesturing towards the bathroom when she hesitated. 'I'll be back in about an hour.'

She had no money to shop. But there was a fluffy cream robe hanging in the bathroom, Sophie remembered. She would just have to put her underwear on after her bath and wear that.

Back in his own suite, Xavier wondered why, of all the doctors in the world, fate had sent him Sophie Ford. Taking a moment to consider, he felt the unmistakable tug of sexual hunger—and it was getting stronger all the time. Why, of all the women in the world, did he want her so badly? And why—when it should have been a simple matter to take her to bed—was he making them both wait? Maybe because the last time he'd seen her she was just a kid. But now... Folding his arms across his chest, Xavier's expression hardened as he eased on to one hip and stared unseeing through the window into the darkness. She was an adult member of the Ford family. She deserved everything she had coming to her. The chase was on, he mused grimly. The champagne aperitif to the full-bodied claret of sex—he loved them both.

The only thing holding him back was that the suggestion of a relationship with a member of the Ford family might be enough to return his mother to her sickbed. He couldn't—he wouldn't risk it. She had suffered enough pain at the hands of the Ford family. But then, what he had planned for Sophie Ford wasn't about to cause his mother a moment's discomfort, Xavier reminded himself.

He ground his jaws together as he conjured up a picture of Sophie naked and demanding in his mind. She wasn't afraid to stand up to him, and she *would* come to his bed, he determined with a harsh smile of anticipation. She was a modern woman—she understood her own needs as well as he knew his own. He would take his pleasure and they would go their separate ways. The irony in the situation appealed to him. It was a relationship that would suit them both—the temptress and the avenger—both finding satisfaction in their own way.

Sophie could have remained soaking in the warm, scented bubbles till night, but a soft female voice coming from the bedroom brought her to her senses. By the time she had climbed out of the Jacuzzi and wrapped herself in the robe, there was no one to be seen. But someone had been in the room, and that someone had left half a dozen carrier bags behind. On top of one of them lay a stiff ivory vellum card printed with the del Condor name in a flourish at the top. Picking it up, Sophie read the bold black handwriting underneath.

Now don't be difficult. Consider these an advance on your wages. Xavier.

She should have known his mother would include a fashionable boutique in her plans. But she should refuse, Sophie thought, viewing the line of carrier bags suspiciously. She *would* refuse, she decided firmly.

It wouldn't hurt to take a peek inside them first.

She couldn't refuse, she realised, swallowing hard.

Letting the robe drop to the floor, she plucked out some underwear first: a cobweb of lace held together by a ribbon of silk. Turning it this way and that, she decided he had got the size about right—and then blushed. Xavier had weighed her up pretty accurately, Sophie realised as she settled her breasts inside the minimalist restraint. The matching thong was something else—it tied at the sides. She made a double knot, and then lost the best part of five minutes and two nails undoing it again. He was hardly going to pounce on her; that wasn't Xavier's style. Looping it once, she turned back to the carrier bags. Wide-legged linen trousers in cream, and a sky-blue silk sleeveless top with a low-cut neck were simply irresistible, if only because she had never imagined in a million years she would get the chance to wear anything so glamorous in her life, let alone in Peru.

It was almost impossible to convince herself she had made a practical choice for eating dinner and discussing business— but she kept the clothes on anyway, and slipped her feet into some simple cream leather mules she found in another bag.

'Are you ready yet? Can I come in?'

'Just a minute.' Dinner and business—and nothing more, Sophie reminded herself fiercely, as she hunted through the remaining bags. Somewhere she had seen some toiletries— basic make-up, a hairbrush...

'Make yourself decent. I'm coming in.'

Groaning with frustration, she emptied all the bags out on the floor and then pounced on what she needed.

She looked like a child on Christmas Day, Xavier thought. His heart lurched in a way he hadn't anticipated as he watched Sophie rooting through clouds of tissue paper and the new clothes he had sent her as a prelude to seduction. 'I'll go out again if you're not quite ready,' he offered casually.

'No, no, that's fine. I'm ready,' Sophie said, hastily gathering everything up. 'This is far too much,' she protested as he walked over to help her. 'I'll never be able to pay you back.'

'Don't be too sure,' Xavier murmured as he picked up the beautiful designer swimming costume she had just dropped on the floor. 'I'll get my money's worth out of you one way or the other.'

'Don't *you* be too sure,' Sophie countered, ignoring the icy fingers that clutched at her spine as their gazes met.

Dinner was possibly the most delicious meal Sophie had ever tasted in her life: a selection of pasta in the lightest, most flavoursome sauces, and salads designed to seduce the palate. There were so many delicacies she couldn't even begin to try them all.

'I hope you have left space for dessert,' Xavier said finally. They were sitting on dining chairs covered in the vibrant local weave at a small table next to the window on her open-fronted veranda with flickering candles as their only light.

'I'm not sure I could,' Sophie admitted, dabbing her lips with the huge linen napkin.

'But you must,' Xavier insisted, ringing a bell.

While the earlier courses were being removed he turned the conversation to medical matters as he had promised. Sophie felt her defences wavering. Xavier's passion for the project was infectious, and the *semifreddo* concoction of moist, light sponge cake and ice cream he had ordered to finish the meal was irresistible too, she mused happily, thinking herself foolish for ever doubting his intentions. He had his ghosts from the past, sure, but under it all he was still Xavier—and a brilliant doctor now. And who would have followed him to Peru if he hadn't been straightforward…trustworthy… For some reason her mind switched to the thought of him choosing her underwear.

'Good?' he murmured.

Could he read minds too? 'Absolutely perfect.' She risked the *double entendre*.

'You never answered the question I put to you in the truck regarding your relationship status.'

Sophie came to with a jolt as he took her off guard. 'I did,' she argued. 'I told you then it was none of your business. It's still none of your business.'

'So, nothing too serious then,' he said, capturing her glance with his dangerous blue eyes.

'I didn't say that.'

'You didn't have to.'

'And you know that, how?' she demanded.

'Quite simple.' He tossed his napkin aside. 'No man, having captured you, would release you immediately to fly to Peru.'

'I am not a bird, Xavier,' Sophie said coolly. 'I make my own decisions when and where I travel. Can we change the subject?' He inclined his head graciously, but not before she had seen the gleam of something in his eyes that made her uneasy.

'Let's talk about your job here,' he said after a few moments.

Sophie relaxed again. But when that conversation faltered he turned back to their sleeping arrangements.

She stiffened immediately. 'You said you were right next door—'

'At Reception, yes,' he agreed. 'Seeing if there were any more rooms available.'

'You mean there aren't any?' Sophie swallowed back her panic.

Xavier shrugged. 'What if I told you that is the case?' He smiled wryly to himself as he waited for her reply. For once in his life the outcome to an invitation to spend the night with him was uncertain. It should have pricked his pride, but it only served to heighten his desire for her. She was almost as skilled at the chase as he was.

Sophie followed his gaze. It was a very large bed. 'No problem at all,' she said, levelling a clear violet blue stare at him. 'You can sleep in the truck.'

Her reply only fuelled his hunger. It amused him too. 'Ouch!' His lips tugged up in a wry smile. 'Do you treat all your men mean? Or is it just me?'

Was he flirting with her? Sophie wondered, wishing she could put a hand round her heart to stop it bouncing about in her chest. 'So, are there any rooms?' she said, in an attempt to steer the conversation out of the danger zone.

'I believe there are one or two free,' he volunteered casually.

Then he stood up, and Sophie's customary defiance faltered. 'You're going?'

'Be ready at dawn.'

Back in his own room, Xavier took a languorous stretch. He was wrapped in a warm blanket of certainty now. Sophie Ford was his for the taking. And what gave his plan added piquancy was the fact that she had proved herself a worthy adversary. This was the type of woman he had waited for all his life—someone who could refresh his jaded palate. And even if fate and his own inclination ensured they had no future together, the present was his to control.

Reaching into the fridge, he pulled out a beer. Only hours before he would have cheerfully sent her home in a crate. Dropping down on to the sofa, Xavier flipped the top on the can and took a deep, cooling draught. His natural inclination was to send women home in style with an expensive gift. It always softened the blow—a small but exquisite piece of jewellery from some place they'd only read about in magazines before, some designer clothes, the private jet to take them out of his life for good. But this was revenge, nothing more; this time he wouldn't bother.

Draining the can, he tossed it into the bin. Only a couple of things prevented it from being the perfect seduction. Sophie's resemblance to her father—and the fact that underneath it all he still felt an edge of regret. Surely not regret for innocence lost? he thought cynically. Then, remembering what a provocative woman Sophie had turned into, he tossed that idea in the trash too. All that mattered now was that sensual anticipation was building inside him to almost un-sustainable levels. But the prize he had in mind would be well worth the wait—for both of them, he'd make sure of it...

CHAPTER FOUR

'I'M GOING to be visiting some pretty wild country,' Xavier warned when they drove off in the truck the next morning. 'It can be dangerous—flash floods, rock falls…'

After a good night's sleep in her sumptuous quarters, Sophie was too relaxed to be ready for anything—least of all Xavier in commanding form. She had been through the assurances that her leg was fully recovered; asked him to thank his mother for the room—which he'd brushed off; thanked him for the clothes—which she had vowed to repay him for, down to the last cunningly concealed hook and eye…and even got over the moment when she almost daydreamed her way into his arms. But, sitting close enough to see his hair was still damp from the shower, and having the citrus scent of the gel he'd used teasing her nostrils, she didn't feel up to having her resolve questioned too.

'Oh, please!'

'What?' he shot back as her challenge rang out.

Sophie bridled to see his eyebrows rise sardonically. 'I am not a little girl, Xavier. I do not need warning about the danger every five minutes. I am quite capable of looking after myself. I am—'

'I am woman?' he enquired mildly, pulling over and stopping the truck at the side of the road.

'That's right,' Sophie agreed fiercely.

'Good. I approve.'

'You do?'

'Get out,' he said, leaving her question hanging. 'This is where we take a break, stretch our legs, eat lunch.'

'Lunch?' She had barely digested breakfast.

'Aren't you hungry?'

51

'Not really.'

'Can't I tempt you?'

Were they still talking about food? Sophie wondered as she climbed down from the truck. It was impossible to tell with Xavier, when his expression revealed so little of the inner workings of his mind.

'You've been spoiled at Del Condor,' he observed dryly, coming to join her.

There were signs of a recent rock-fall at the side of the truck and, though she trod carefully, Sophie trusted her weight to the wrong boulder.

'This is worse than caring for a five-year-old child!' Xavier exclaimed, grabbing hold of her hands to haul her up again.

'Of which you would know such a lot,' Sophie muttered mutinously, shaking him off when he tried to check her over.

'Damage?' he demanded curtly.

'None.'

'Let me see—'

'No!'

Grabbing her shoulders, Xavier swung her round to face him. As they collided, Sophie got the air knocked out of her. Recovering, she meant to get over it, carry on—but as she glanced up at him something very different happened. A ribbon of heat wound around her. And, as she stood motionless in front of him, Xavier ran his palms lightly down her arms from her shoulders to the tips of her fingers so that she trembled beneath his touch like a finely bred mare.

He could have kissed her then, but chose not to. Knowing the hunger was always there for her, like a nagging itch she couldn't reach, was enough for now. It gave him pleasure to see her drawn taut like a bowstring as she waited for him to make a move. Her nipples were like two firm points against his chest, commanding he take them between his lips and suckle. He dismissed the erotic image. It pleased him to be tested. It was good to have this chance to flex his control. Taking Sophie in a firm grip, he held her at arm's length.

But somehow she slipped his grip. There was just enough

time to see the glint of refusal to accept defeat in her eyes before she lashed her arms around his neck. Accepting the challenge, Xavier dragged her back into his arms with a growl of triumph.

For one fleeting moment Sophie felt the warm, firm touch of his lips, but then she felt the heat of his arousal, the hard pressure of his desire, and pitched back in terror. 'No!'

There was such a choking note of panic in her voice Xavier stepped back, thrusting his hands in the air, palms raised towards her, signalling his intention to do nothing more.

Once again she had surprised him, he realised grimly. He would accept his many faults, but misjudging a woman's responses had never been one of them before now.

Reading his proud, closed face, Sophie knew Xavier thought she was leading him on—tempting, teasing, and finally throwing herself at him. How could she deny it, when only ghosts from the past had stopped her, taking the heat of her passion in their icy fingers and squeezing the life out of it? 'I'm sorry. The shock of the fall,' she said awkwardly. She was emotionally drained…emotionally bankrupt.

'Help me gather some wood,' he said, turning away. 'We need to cook food, heat coffee.'

Sophie was happy to hear the lack of emotion in his voice and lose herself in the mundane tasks. But there was no escape—from Xavier, or from the embarrassing position she had put herself in, and when they were finally settled down to eat the food only balled in her throat like a fist.

'It will be a long time until supper,' he said curtly, without sparing her a glance.

Sophie tried again, chewing repeatedly, tasting nothing. Her mouth might have been filled with sawdust.

'Here, take a drink,' he said, passing her a cup.

Making sure their fingers didn't touch, Sophie took hold of it, gulping down the burning liquid, and then attacking the food again until she managed to dispose of it. But her mind was full of Xavier—the almost kiss, the feel of his hard mouth softening as their lips touched. How was it possible to feel such strong attraction and at the same time such fear? Fear had made her push him away: a fear that wasn't even her own—an inherited fear, a fear learned in childhood. Averting her face, she grimaced angrily. She only had to remember her father to know the answer. He had been handsome too in his foppish way—handsome and selfish and cruel. Her mind just didn't seem able to accept that a man as good-looking as Xavier—a man so charismatic, and so blatantly sexual—could be any different. So, while part of her longed for his skilful touch, a touch she knew would bring pleasure beyond her wildest dreams, another side of her insisted that skill had to be honed somehow—it didn't just come out of the blue.

And when he tired of her—what then? She knew the answer to that too: disillusionment. The string of lovers, the broken promises, the drinking—*violence*— She shuddered, remembering. And almost worse, if such a thing was possible, the betrayal down at the very core of the relationship followed by loneliness, bewilderment, and complete and utter loss of self. Loss of self-esteem was one thing—maybe she could recover from that, but loss of self, loss of who you were…who you were before… She had seen her mother take each one of those steps without complaint—without even feeling humiliation. Her father had done far too good a job for that.

By the time Xavier took the plate and mug away and told her it was time to go, Sophie was so immersed in the past she didn't move at first. Ignoring her garbled protests, Xavier just grabbed hold of her hands and hauled her to her feet.

'You look wrecked,' he observed. 'You're no use to the project in this state. You can doze in the truck while I drive. As your boss I'm laying down the law. We'll reach the clinic by nightfall, and then I'm putting you to bed.'

Sophie heard nothing more—wasn't even aware that she mewled out loud like a kitten with its paw stuck in a door.

'I'm not interested in your excuses, so don't even bother,' he said grimly, steering her towards the truck.

'I can manage by myself,' Sophie insisted, rallying fast.

'Maybe,' Xavier agreed, his voice rising over hers. 'But why the hell should you?'

His outburst, accompanied by a frustrated move of stiff, angry fingers through his hair, surprised them both. They stood in silence for a moment beside the closed passenger door of the truck. Then, leaning across her, Xavier opened it and gestured with a curt dip of his head that she should climb inside.

'I'm allowed to open doors for you once in a while,' he growled as Sophie moved past him. 'I promise not to take it as a sign of weakness if you let me.'

When they reached the clinic everywhere was silent and deserted, and the only light came from a watery moon half hidden in cloud. Unlocking the door, Xavier flicked on the light switches and ushered her inside.

'I'll show you where everything is tomorrow,' he said, taking her straight through to the bedroom. 'Have you brought any night clothes with you?'

'I brought my new clothes from the ranch.'

'Great,' Xavier murmured to himself. 'A silk negligée and a flimsy slip of a nightgown—'

Bought for seduction? Sophie thought, while Xavier gave her the distinct impression there would be no use for them now.

'I should have an old T-shirt you can have,' he said, confirming her thoughts. 'And tomorrow I'll have your rucksack and the rest of your things brought up here from base.'

He paused with his hand up on the doorframe. 'Do you need anything else before I turn in?'

Yes, you. Sophie held her breath as his lips moved in the shadow of a smile. She was determined to conquer the fear. She would not allow it to rule her life. Xavier wouldn't touch her tonight—maybe he never would again. Normally she could feel his sexual intentions coming off him in waves—

they lapped around her, crashed over her—but right now, the tide was out. 'You mentioned a T-shirt.'

He dipped his head briefly, acknowledging her request, and then backed out of the door.

One more chance, Sophie thought, taking a deep, steadying breath. Picturing the two of them naked, filling the small room with the sounds of passion, made her ache for him all the more. If she didn't take the initiative she was destined to spend the night alone...the rest of her time in Peru alone. Sophie gave a low, hollow laugh—the rest of her life alone.

'I'll leave the T-shirt out here for you on the hook. Call me if you need anything more.'

Sophie came alert immediately, but the door had already closed behind him again.

Getting off the bed, she reached an arm through a crack in the door, felt around and retrieved the T-shirt. Predictably, it drowned her. Fluffing out her hair and moistening her lips, she arranged herself in what she hoped was an attractive pose, cross-legged on the narrow bed, and then called him back in. She had almost given up on him getting back to her at all when the door swung open.

'I've got something for you,' he said, remaining half in and half out of the room.

'Come in, I'm quite decent—' For now.

Xavier moved a little deeper into the confined space but, crucially, he left the door open.

'Brr... Don't you feel a draught?' Sophie hinted.

'Not particularly.' His lips tugged down in a negative.

'So. What have you got for me?' She wasn't good at this, Sophie realised. The sultry voice might work for some women—but not for her!

'Just this,' Xavier said, appearing not to notice any change in her behaviour.

In fact, he'd barely looked at her once since coming into the room, she registered. If she was going to get this seduction off the ground at all, she was going to have to try a lot harder. Then he handed her a small, battery-powered lantern.

'It's just a night-light, in case you need it.'

Oh, great! This was worse than she had thought. Now he was treating her like a child. Words of thanks for the night-light stalled on her lips as he stretched out a hand towards her.

'Why did you cut your hair?' He pushed one of the annoying strands off her face and even that was enough to induce a shower of sensation.

'My first year at med school… There was no time—'

'Too bad,' he cut in softly. 'I liked it long. You should grow it again.'

Sophie's emotions surged on to a new level. She tried not to notice how strong his arms were beneath the shading of dark hair, or to see the muscles working beneath the broad black leather wristband he wore in memory of his brother, or hear the rhythmical stroke of his watch as it counted down the seconds to the moment he'd leave—if she didn't make a move. She had no idea how he would react. His very masculine appetites were in no doubt, but his pride was something else. Xavier had made his move on her, and she had rejected him once…twice…too many times, that was for sure.

Anticipation was bearing down on every part of her like countless stroking, teasing fingers. His voice was so soft…so soft and seductive…and she was seduced. She moistened her lips. The only thing missing now was Xavier's active participation in the seduction. She had to let him know—show him that he must forget what had happened between them earlier. But what to do, and when—how to do it? Fast…slow…now? Should she reach for the buttons on his shirt? She felt her heart begin to dance around in her chest as she prepared to make her move. But then he made it easy for her—tucking some hair behind her ear as she looked up at him. Reaching for his hand, Sophie caught hold of it and, bringing it to her lips, she quite deliberately drew it lower, encouraging Xavier to nurse her breast through the fabric of his old T-shirt. He took control immediately, his thumb finding the erect and highly sensitised nipple tip, while his fingers moulded the generous curves appreciatively. But he was still standing— that was wrong, surely. Drawing Xavier with her, Sophie slowly sank back on to the thin pillows.

With a growl of triumph, he lay at her side, capturing her neglected breast in one strong hand while his mouth closed over the painfully extended nipple of the first through the fine cotton fabric. Sophie bucked involuntarily as his warm, moist breath coaxed every one of her nerve-endings to the surface of her pale, delicate skin. And then his firm lips increased her pleasure, bringing her nipple deep into his hot mouth to be rolled and stroked by his tongue.

And now she was shuddering, trembling, moaning, every part of her suffused with feeling. The places he touched were only centres of sensation—sensation that drowned her body in thought-robbing waves. It was a barrage of sensation she had no idea how to withstand. Xavier's free hand was meshed in the hair at the back of her head, his fingers controlling, strong, and demanding—and when he finally dragged himself away from her breast and moved up the bed towards her, his eyes were blazing with passion and…

'No!'

She cried out just that one word, but it divided them like a whiplash. In the space of a heartbeat she was off the bed and pressed up against the wall, arms lashed around her body for protection. The small size of the room meant she could only get a foot or two away from him. It had to be enough— it was as far as she could get.

Xavier's powerful body coiled, sprang and straightened in practically the same instant. And now he was towering over her, taking all the light, all the space, all the air. They were inches apart, but it might have been miles. Sophie could see nothing in his face but anger and contempt.

'What the hell do you think you're doing?' he raged.

But, as his fists shot out on either side of her head to pin her to the wall, she let out a wounded cry and sank down on to the floor at his feet, covering her head with her arms in terror.

'Sophie?'

His voice seemed to come from far away and was little more than a whisper.

'Sophie,' he said again, hunkering down on the floor in front of her. 'Sophie, what is it?' He wouldn't touch her—not yet.

He wouldn't touch her ever again, Sophie thought, certain she was right.

She was so pale. She had to be exhausted, Xavier reasoned—though she was doing a great impression of being terrified. Maybe she wasn't acting! However incredible it seemed to him, there was always the possibility that she really didn't know what to do—and for some reason expected to be punished for her lack of experience. The thought sickened him. Could she be frightened of him? he wondered incredulously. His whole psyche flinched as he turned the possibility over in his mind. He couldn't even entertain the thought. Frightening women was for bullies—inadequates. Looking at her again, he felt a sudden and totally unexpected rush of tenderness. But he couldn't afford to let her in—to let anyone in—and Sophie Ford, of all people? Chipping away at his heart until it was mush for her to trample over? No thank you. And wouldn't that be a great gift for his mother? Look who I've brought to see you, *Mama*. No way!

He looked at her again, really looked at her—and this time with the eyes of a physician. She had a deep-seated problem, all right, somewhere in her past. Xavier frowned as he mulled it over. He had encountered physical symptoms before that had their roots in some hidden cause. It seemed to him as if Sophie was serving her own life sentence—for what, he didn't know yet, but he would find out. Maybe she just got tired of being a player—and that was something he could understand, Xavier mused cynically. He was getting soft, he told himself, dragging his gaze away from her. 'I'll get you something,' he said, standing up again. 'Something to help you sleep. Why don't you get back into bed.'

'Yes. Thank you,' Sophie managed evenly, hearing the

doctor in his voice. She waited until the door shut behind him and then got to her feet and climbed into bed.

Xavier brought her some warm milk to go with the night-light, and tried to keep a healthy dose of cynicism at the forefront of his mind as he gave it to her. Was the ice around his heart melting? he wondered as he watched her—hands wrapped around the mug as she drank, face burrowed into it. His lips tugged down in a sardonic half-smile. Or was this life's finest irony? When there should have only been space for revenge in his heart, had Sophie Ford discovered an empty corner and claimed it as her own? 'Ah, what the hell,' he murmured under his breath and, leaning over, he impulsively brushed a kiss against her forehead. To seduce her, enjoy her and discard her before their relationship could cause any damage depended on Sophie playing along—and, quite suddenly, he wasn't so sure of anything as far as Sophie Ford was concerned.

On his way out of the door Xavier stopped. He *was* getting soft, he realised grimly, catching sight of the photograph of Sophie's mother she had found time to tuck inside the frame of the mirror. She'd only been in the room five minutes, and already she was sticking up photographs of her family—would her father's be next?

Stay with what you know best, Doctor, Xavier told himself, hardening his heart. Casting a professional eye over Sophie, he took comfort in the fact that he never had been able to see a problem without wanting to find the solution to it. That had been the basis of his attraction to the medical profession. And that was his motivation now, he told himself firmly, taking hold of Sophie's exposed arm and tucking it inside the sleeping bag.

'Sleep well,' he said. 'I'll see you in the morning.' And, switching off the light, he left the room.

The instant Sophie's head hit the pillow she fell deeply asleep, but when she woke the next morning she heard Xavier moving around outside the room and, climbing out of the sleeping bag, she quickly pulled on her clothes and went out to join him. She was determined to behave as if nothing untoward had happened the night before. It was the only way they were going to be able to work together—and, to her relief, the look on his face told her Xavier had drawn the same conclusion.

'What time is it?' She hadn't got round to resetting her wristwatch on to the new time zone, and could only guess by the faint pink still lining the horizon that it was shortly after dawn.

'Time for a swim,' he said casually, raking his hair in a way she was becoming accustomed to, so that it stood up in short, dark spikes.

'Swim?'

'Why not?' Alone, to give him the chance to think over what had happened the previous night, had been his original plan—but now she was here…

'The water around here must come down from the glaciers.'

'So?' Xavier demanded with a wry look of enquiry.

'So, it will be freezing,' Sophie pointed out reasonably.

'Have you grown soft since you used to come to Spain to ski in the Sierra Nevada mountains, Sophie?'

She hid her surprise. The past was not an entirely forbidden topic for him, as she had supposed.

'I can still remember you rolling in the snow in just your underwear when you were a little girl.'

'That was different,' Sophie protested.

'How?'

'I didn't know any better back then.'

'You seemed to enjoy it at the time,' he observed casually. 'Why don't you come with me now and see if you've got any of that pluck left?' He had told himself he wasn't going to goad her ever again. He was going to keep his distance from now on—professional interest only. The last thing he had wanted was to bring that glint back into her eyes. Xavier groaned inwardly—maybe they had just known each other too long. It was already there.

'Forget it!' Sophie exclaimed, meaning just the opposite. A swim sounded great—especially if it helped to clear the air between them after last night.

She had driven him to the limits last night, Xavier realised, angling a stare at her. But anything—anything on earth was preferable to ever seeing her cowering at his feet again. Even this, he accepted ruefully, seeing her chin tilt up for combat. 'Forgotten how to swim?' he demanded, intentionally ratcheting up the challenge.

'No.'

'I'll take good care of you.'

Sophie squared her shoulders as she glared at him, all thoughts of warm sleeping bags forgotten. 'You think I need it?'

'Yes.'

There was so much going on behind that dark, challenging gaze. Quite unexpectedly, a shower of sensation left no part of her untouched.

Easing on to one hip, Xavier threw her an insolent stare. 'Chicken?'

'Certainly not!'

'I am woman,' he mocked. 'Or does that not extend as far as being as hardy as the male of the species?'

Sophie blazed back a look. 'I see you are determined to goad me.'

Xavier contented himself with a lazy shrug. 'The sun's coming out. It will soon be warm. Remember how hot it was yesterday?'

'But the water will still be freezing.' And she was shivering already, but not from the cold, Sophie realised.

'You are chicken,' he said, starting to move away.

'We'll see about that,' Sophie countered determinedly. 'I'm coming with you.'

'How far did you say it was?' she demanded when they had been trudging up scree that slid away beneath her feet for what seemed like eternity. But when they crested the steep hill Sophie saw why Xavier had insisted on climbing so far. A blemish-free pool of water, surrounded by lush vegetation, stretched out in front of them like an oasis in the mountains.

'Worth the climb?' Xavier demanded, turning to look at her.

'More than worth it,' she was forced to admit. 'It's really beautiful.' Sophie shook her head in awe as she stared around. She knew many deep lakes had been carved out by the glaciers, but had never expected to visit one—let alone swim in one. They had climbed even higher than she had imagined, but still the towering crags surrounding them seemed to stretch away into infinity. The sun was blindingly bright and already quite hot on her face as she peered upwards trying to see where the snow-capped peaks ended and the puffball clouds littering the clear blue sky began.

'Feeling OK?' Xavier said, casting a professional eye over her. 'You did prepare properly for this trip? We're at a really high altitude now.'

'Of course.'

'In the gym?' he pressed, refusing to be satisfied by the brevity of her answer.

'That too,' Sophie admitted, knowing she was going to have to give him the whole nine yards. 'But I've been taking supplements like iron and Gingko Biloba too, to boost the supply of oxygen to my brain. Don't,' she warned, when she saw the hint of a smile tugging at his lips.

'Starting when?' Xavier said, reverting swiftly back to doctor mode.

'A couple of weeks ago.'

'Quality brands?'

'Of course,' Sophie confirmed, knowing there was a wide spectrum of homeopathic remedies, some of which fell off the poor end of the chart in quite spectacular fashion.

'OK, then.'

He appeared satisfied with her answers. 'After you,'

Sophie invited, staring out across the mirrored surface of the aquamarine lake.

'Let's take a moment first,' Xavier suggested, sucking in a deep breath.

He looked almost relaxed for the first time since she had arrived, Sophie thought, as they stood listening to the silence. They might have been the only two people in the world. 'The air feels as if—'

'We're the first people ever to breathe it in,' Xavier finished for her.

'Pretty much.' She moved away from him to stand on a ledge overhanging the water. 'Maybe we are the first people ever to step on this piece of ground,' she said, turning back to look at him.

Xavier was surprised at the amount of pleasure it gave him to see Sophie looking so happy. There were no dark shadows marring her beauty, and the anticipation in her face had brightened her eyes to the shade of a wild pansy. 'Come on,' he said, before his feelings ran away with him. 'We have a lot of work to do today—there's not much time for swimming—and perhaps I should warn you that the last one in the water gets to sort out the filing system.'

The fact that he could tease her was a real breakthrough, Sophie thought, starting to pull off her clothes. 'I hope you've got nimble fingers.' She looked around to see he was already toeing off his boots and fingering the buckle on his belt.

'And I thought the last thing you wanted was to be stuck back at base,' he taunted when she ground to a sudden halt. And then realisation struck. 'You did bring something to wear?'

Sophie reddened. 'Did you?' When their eyes clashed she noticed Xavier's were dancing with laughter. His shirt was off already, and he was grabbing hold of the edge of the tight-fitting top he wore beneath. His jeans were gaping open and the top had ridden up on one side to reveal a tantalising glimpse of hard, bronzed flesh, with just the suggestion of some shadowy dark hair, and he showed no sign of stopping.

'Would you like me to undress you?' he threatened, pausing to capture her glance in his hot, amused stare.

Redoubling her efforts, Sophie tugged her jumper over her head, and then threw herself down on the ground to drag off her boots.

'What about a ten-second start?' Xavier suggested.

He had black swimming shorts under his jeans—shorts that showed a lot of powerful thigh, Sophie noticed. Dragging her gaze away, she shrugged. 'If you think you need it.'

'I should throw you in for that,' he threatened, a darkly wicked smile tugging at the corner of his lips.

'You'd have to catch me first.' Sophie moved out of reach, but kept him in her eye-line. The sight of Xavier's body was a revelation. Did men really come shaped like that? In the course of her work she'd seen plenty—but those broad shoulders, washboard stomachs and rippling muscles had definitely escaped her.

Every time she hesitated he kept on coming closer, keeping her on the move so that she had to pull her socks off on the hop. Down to her bra and thong—which, thanks to Xavier's choice in underwear, didn't offer much in the way of concealment—Sophie knew she couldn't hang around if she wanted to get in before she was thrown in. The excitement was kicking her heart into overdrive and there was hardly a chance to brace herself before she stood poised on the edge to dive in. But the cool water felt fantastic after the exertion of the climb. The heat of the sun, not to mention an overheated body, had left her feeling all keyed up, and it was great to yield to the refreshing change in temperature.

She remained submerged for quite a while, and when she finally swooped to the surface it was like streaking through a faintly blue, liquid ice cube. As her face broke the surface she gave a great gasping splutter of relief and excitement.

'Better?' Xavier called across.

'Much better,' Sophie shouted back. The sun was comfortingly warm on her cheeks and, as she began to power across the smooth surface towards him, she saw him spring out. He stood for a moment in silhouette against the sky and then, diving back in again, he swam to her side.

That image would be branded on her mind for ever, Sophie realised, keeping her appreciation to herself. Wasn't cold meant to affect men? Apparently not, in Xavier's case! Either that or he was exceptionally blessed. The wet shorts had clung to him like a second skin. She closed her eyes, but the picture remained just as vivid, almost doubly enjoyable in her mind's eye, like a single frame from a film frozen in time. 'You swim well,' she said innocently, keeping a little distance between them as they trod water together.

'We always did swim well, both of us,' Xavier reminded her, tossing his head to clear the water from his eyes and ears, 'or had you forgotten, Sophie?'

No, she hadn't forgotten, Sophie thought, reminiscing for a moment as she absorbed how attractive he looked with his dark hair clinging wetly to his face, emphasising his incredible bone structure. Water droplets glinted in the sunshine like thousands of diamonds on the tips of his dark hair. Suddenly conscious that she was staring, she looked away and glanced down, only to find that the crystal clear water revealed far more of him than she was ready to see close up. Feeling a rush of excitement, she whirled around in the water, gave a shriek of challenge, and began to race towards the opposite bank. But Xavier was too fast for her and overtook her without any trouble, arriving first beneath the glittering waterfall that fed the pool.

'You don't get away from me that easily,' he informed her as he caught hold of her and dragged her against him. 'And now,' he said sternly, 'a forfeit, I think.'

He felt so warm, yet Sophie was shivering. Panic and excitement combined, she realised, knowing her nipples were hard against his arm—surely he must feel them...

'My forfeit,' he reminded her in a husky drawl. He was so close she could feel his body heat warming her, seeping through her like a spell until her legs seemed to bind with his of their own accord.

'No, Xavier,' Sophie protested half-heartedly. It was she who had him in her clutches, her legs wound around his. He wasn't even holding her…she could get away whenever she wanted to.

'No?' he murmured, drawing her close, his hand, his arm, barely touching her waist… And then he was forced to grab an overhanging branch to keep them both afloat.

Looking up, Sophie saw his shoulder muscles bunch as he took their weight. Their faces were close, too close. 'Xavier—'

'What?' His warm breath was on her ear, and it sent a flurry of vibrations shimmering through her. Her thoughts stalled as she took in the spread of his shoulders, the power in his chest. And then he shifted slightly so that one hard thigh brushed her intimately.

The sudden contact took her by surprise and she jerked away, but he caught her close again. 'That was an accident,' he said steadily.

'I—I know…I know that.' She grew calm again, listening to the water lapping on the bank and the rustle of the leaves above their heads. She could feel his breath warming her neck. His dark eyes were watching her, and his lips were very close. Turning her face up to him, Sophie closed her eyes, mouth parted.

Xavier's lips were just as she remembered them, warm and smooth and firm. His face was damp, and the stubble on his unshaven chin was a new and unexpected delight as it rasped against her tender skin. As a ragged sigh escaped her and she moved towards him, seeking the full warmth of his body on hers, Xavier deepened the kiss, his tongue moving persuasively against her own. With one hand he held on to the branch above their heads, and he kept the other hand well away from her.

The branch snapped without warning, a giant report like a shot from a gun. It surprised them both. Sophie shrieked, while Xavier captured her tight as they dropped beneath the water. Bringing her quickly to the surface again, he lifted her up on the bank. 'Your clothes,' he pointed out, dropping down on the ground by her side.

He was laughing. She was naked. Somehow her bra had come off, and the ties on the tiny thong he had bought her at the Rancho del Condor had come undone.

'Here—let me,' Xavier offered, still laughing at the episode. He rolled over on the ground, catching the ribbons of her thong in his hand as he went.

'Get away!' Sophie warned nervously, clambering to her feet and covering herself with her hands.

Springing to his feet, Xavier faced her. 'What's wrong with you?' he asked in a low, intense voice.

For a moment neither of them spoke. Then, very slowly, Xavier began to shake his head, running strong, tanned fingers through his tousled hair. 'Oh, no,' he said on a soft moan, 'you can't do this to me, Sophie.'

'Can't do what?' Sophie exclaimed defensively.

'Lead me on. Tease me like this. You put a name to it.'

She saw he was growing really angry. His mouth had flattened into a hard line, and his eyes were full of intensity and passion. As he moved towards her, Sophie instinctively backed away. Catching her heel in a tree root, she lost her balance and tumbled backwards.

Xavier snatched out his hands to catch her, but they only closed on the air. When he saw what she had done his face turned ashen. Instead of putting her hands behind her back to break the fall, she had put them up to her face as if she thought he was going to hit her.

'Sophie!' He expelled her name on a ragged breath, swooping down to take hold of her.

As his arms closed around her Sophie grew rigid. Putting her hands up to his chest, she tried to push him away, but he was too strong for her. And yet it was the strength of a rock to cling to in a storm, not the strength of the wave that would have dashed her against it. Little by little, she began to unwind and as she let go the tears soon followed until, sheltering within Xavier's embrace, she began to sob with shock and relief.

'Sophie, Sophie, don't cry,' Xavier implored. Reaching out a hand, he managed to grab his own shirt and when he had wrapped her in it he brought her close and rocked her gently like a baby in his arms, dropping kisses on her head until gradually she grew calm again. 'How could you think I would ever hurt you?' he murmured against the soft tumble of her hair. It was such a revelation to him, and yet he couldn't imagine how he'd ever missed it. She was frightened of him—frightened he might hit her, abuse her. Xavier squeezed his eyes shut against the truth. It was too awful to contemplate. She was so vulnerable, so damaged, and he had been blind.

. So this was what he'd come to, Xavier mused bitterly. The capacity to care had deserted him on the day his brother had been killed—he knew that. But surely his intuition hadn't left him at the same time? For some reason sex was a stumbling block he hadn't anticipated where Sophie was concerned. She was a feisty and successful woman—vibrant and self-assured in every other area of her life. A worthy sparring partner, or how else could he have contemplated a casual relationship with her? And she must have aroused feelings in other men. He certainly desired her like no other woman he could remember. She desired him too, he was sure of it. So there was no problem there; no problem other than her inability to let herself go physically—to place her trust in him.

When he was sure she was calm, Xavier collected up Sophie's clothes and then got dressed behind a huge boulder he adopted as an improvised dressing room. He emerged a few minutes later, rubbing his hair vigorously on a towel. 'We should get back. We don't want to be late for our first clinic together.'

They shared a look, and Sophie was grateful he didn't ply her with questions. Several onion-skins of mistrust had peeled away, she realised. She had been exposed and vulnerable and Xavier had shed his bitter exterior, if only for a moment, to help her, revealing a very different side to his character.

But then she reminded herself that Xavier was a very good doctor. He had identified a problem and embarked upon a cure. There was nothing more to his gesture of kindness than that.

CHAPTER FIVE

As THEY approached the clinic, Sophie saw crowds of people milling about in the previously deserted yard. The moment they caught sight of Xavier they began smiling and waving.

'Your patients await you,' she remarked softly.

'Go to work, Doctor,' Xavier said, giving her a light nudge of encouragement.

A wave of emotion swept over Sophie, seeing so many people waiting for them in the hot sun. The fact they would be working together side by side for the first time was secondary, and she was determined to stay focused. With a quick smile she took the keys from Xavier and hurried ahead to unlock the door of the clinic.

For the next couple of hours they didn't have time to exchange a single word. They were sharing a surgery with a small treatment room off it, and in a rare gap between patients Sophie wiped her forehead on her sleeve and glanced across. During the course of the morning she had the chance to discover that all Xavier's better qualities were intact, at least as far as his patients were concerned. Nothing was too much trouble for him. Noticing he had run short of supplies, she left her post briefly to go and stock up for him.

'You didn't need to do that,' Xavier murmured when she returned, concentrating on the small wound he was dressing on a young girl's arm.

'I wanted to.'

Still concentrating on his work, his lips pulled down in a wry show of surprise. 'Well, thank you.'

In spite of all her self-administered warnings, the grin he slanted at her sent Sophie's pulse rate soaring.

'I'll get that,' he offered as the telephone rang in the reception area when she had just sat down.

'Oh, OK,' Sophie agreed. Sharing the workload with Xavier was running like clockwork. They were perfect partners—at work at least, she realised wryly, turning to meet her next patient.

It wasn't until much later in the day, after they had seen their last patient, that Sophie had the opportunity to meet some more members of the medical team when they arrived back from their visits to the outlying areas. After freshening up, they assembled in the dining area with drinks and snacks to relax. She found them all friendly and welcoming—with one exception, a striking-looking woman a little older than herself.

'This is Dr Anna Groes from Denmark,' Xavier said casually, introducing Sophie to the statuesque blonde.

She would have had to be numb from the neck up not to feel the bolt of electricity that shot from Anna Groes to Xavier—singeing her on the way, Sophie thought, trying to tell herself she was imagining it. But Xavier walked away before she could make any more of it. He had been tense ever since the telephone call earlier, Sophie remembered, admiring the broad sweep of his shoulders as he crossed the room.

'Dr Ford—'

Sophie turned back to Anna Groes. It was like shaking hands with a cheese slice. The Danish doctor's hand was cold, smooth, and limp, her stare penetrating and as cold as her hand. It left Sophie feeling as if she was being systematically dissected, analysed and judged.

'You should take some time off, Xavier,' the Danish doctor said in a provocative drawl when he came back to them.

Sophie felt her hackles rising—a feeling that only increased when Anna Groes dismissed her with one careless blink of her sooty-black lashes. 'You know what they say in your country about all work and no play—'

'But no one could ever accuse Xavier of being dull,' Sophie cut in.

'I see the new recruit has got the measure of you already, Xavier.' The woman's tone managed to imply that Sophie was junior in rank to her and therefore of no consequence.

'Sophie and I know each other from way back,' Xavier explained, keeping his voice neutral.

'Ah, I see—'

'No you don't, Anna. You don't see at all,' Xavier warned, killing the conversation stone dead. 'Come on, Sophie, let's get out of here.'

'Why, I—'

'Now,' he said icily.

Xavier's black mood had obviously been precipitated by the encounter with Anna Groes, Sophie thought, when he slammed the clinic door behind them and stalked off ahead of her. She had no idea where he was taking her, and had no inclination to ask—anywhere away from Anna would suit her just fine.

They were halfway across the almost deserted yard when a touch on Sophie's sleeve made her stop. But it was just the young girl Xavier had treated for a wound on her arm, holding out a piece of beautiful and distinctive Peruvian cloth.

'What does she want?' Sophie called after Xavier, smiling down at the child.

'She wants to give it to you,' Xavier said as he turned from Sophie to speak to the child's parents.

'But I can't,' Sophie whispered urgently, catching hold of Xavier's sleeve to get his attention. 'I don't have anything to give her in return.'

'I think her family might disagree with that,' he murmured, flashing a smile at them.

'But they have so little—'

'And they want you to have this,' he said firmly, taking the fabric from Sophie's hands and tossing it round her neck. 'It's beautiful, and special to them. It would be impolite of you to refuse.'

He sounded almost angry as he turned back to speak to them again, Sophie thought uncomfortably. Of course it was rude of her to ignore the family when they had given her such a beautiful gift. Turning to them, she said, *'Gracias, muchas gracias,'* as she held the soft woven fabric to her cheek.

To her surprise, the child took the long piece of material away from her and, taking hold of Xavier's hand, gestured that he and Sophie must hold hands.

'Oh, no, I—'

'Take it,' Xavier warned softly.

'OK,' Sophie agreed, uncomfortable suddenly. She pinned a smile to her face as the little girl solemnly wrapped the piece of vivid red fabric around their clasped hands to a round of applause from her family. 'Oh, no, I'm—'

'What?' Xavier demanded, keeping a pleasant expression on his face while he continued to murmur in her ear. 'Engaged to another man?'

'What?'

'Poor Henry Whitland,' he drawled softly, smiling and bowing at the same time to the young girl's family as the child, having shyly removed the piece of fabric that bound them together, placed it in Sophie's hands.

'How do you know—?'

'About Henry? Simple. He telephoned to see how things are going—' Xavier broke off to make a derisive sound. 'They're going pretty well, I told him. I should get her into bed any day now.'

'Xavier, listen to me—'

Sophie could only watch in an agony of frustration as he turned on his heel and strode off, but she still made sure to express her thanks to each member of the family in turn. There was no way she was going to allow Xavier to get to her. But he had almost reached the truck…

The young girl's mother gently removed the shawl from Sophie's hands, where she was twisting it into a string, and arranged it around her shoulders. Then, squeezing Sophie's arm, she turned her around and gestured with her head in Xavier's direction.

'Oh, no, I—'

But the woman was insistent and, while Sophie was hesitating, Xavier came to a halt and swung around.

'Well, Dr Ford?' he demanded impatiently. 'Are you thinking of joining me any time today? Or do you take your medical duties as lightly as your personal responsibilities?'

Sophie bit down on the angry words that sprang to her lips. The child's mother was standing right next to her. It left her with little option when the older woman gave her an encouraging nudge in Xavier's direction.

As Xavier gunned the engine into life, Sophie steadied herself with her hand against the door. Without that mention of her medical duties she wouldn't have agreed to accompany him, and when he made no attempt to explain where they were going she asked him outright.

'Some of the areas we service are inaccessible by road,' he revealed tersely. 'There's a pick-up point. You need to know about it.'

So there was a drive, and then a journey on foot. Inevitably, they would spend quite a bit of time together—time she didn't intend to pass with the subject of Henry hanging over her head like the sword of Damocles. 'About Henry—'

'Not now.'

'It's as good a time as any.'

'I'm not prepared to discuss personal matters on my time,' Xavier said pointedly.

Bringing personal matters into the workplace had never been her way—but this was different; the lines were blurred.

'I didn't believe him at first—'

The cruel edge in Xavier's voice broke into Sophie's introspection. She watched as he turned in his seat to drag out her jacket from the back.

'So I went looking for proof.'

'I don't know what Henry could possibly have told you.'

'Oh, really?' Xavier stopped without warning at the side of the road. 'Well, I think you're a lying little—'

'Stop it!' Sophie exclaimed angrily, shocked by the sudden halt. 'There's no need to frighten me to death with bad driving—just explain what you mean. If you give me a chance, I'll tell you about Henry—and then you can apologise.'

'This time you're the one who has to apologise,' Xavier cut in. Holding her gaze, he undid the button on the top pocket of her jacket, pulling out the antique amethyst ring Henry Whitland had given to Sophie before she left England.

She was her father's daughter all right, he thought, as he watched Sophie's reaction. She didn't cry and wail and beg him to forgive her. She thought it all through while she worked out her next move. She was playing for a lot more than just an amethyst ring, after all, he mused cynically. The Martinez Bordiu fortune was well worth a wager. 'Playing for bigger stakes than this now, aren't you?' he suggested derisively, brandishing the ring in front of her face.

'That's not worthy of you, Xavier—and neither is going through my things.'

His pride took a direct hit. But he was still going to get that explanation. 'Henry said he gave you this ring. I didn't have far to look. Here—you'd better keep it safe; it must mean a lot to you.'

'It's a friendship ring, nothing more,' Sophie said firmly. 'And if you'll let me, I'll tell you about Henry.'

'Save it,' Xavier said tersely. 'Your private life's your own business. I'm only interested in how you perform as a doctor.' And that was the only way to think of her, Xavier warned himself fiercely. Anything else had been madness from the start.

'I'm going to tell you about Henry one way or the other,' Sophie insisted calmly. 'So why don't you just drive, and I'll tell you about him as we go? And then,' she added with steel in her voice, 'you can apologise.'

She had nerve, Xavier reflected grimly. But he wouldn't fall for her so-convincing act again. To think that he, who never let anyone in, had so nearly made an exception for Sophie Ford!

'If I can't talk to you, then I don't think we can work together,' Sophie continued evenly, 'and you need me here at least until the new doctors arrive.'

Xavier ground his jaws together. Not only did she have nerve, she had an unerring aim when it came to his Achilles' heel. Unfortunately, she was right. Until more medical staff arrived from Europe the project was in danger of being seriously understaffed.

'Henry and I have a very open relationship,' Sophie began evenly.

An *open* relationship? What was that supposed to mean? His senses wanted it to mean one thing while reason told him her use of the phrase was misleading. Either way, it suggested her supposed fear of men wasn't as strong as she had led him to believe. And that meant the chase was back on. 'I don't want to hear,' he said impatiently, starting the engine up.

'Tough,' Sophie said, forcing a level stare on Xavier's fierce features, 'because you're going to hear what I have to say, whether you want to or not. The arrangement I have with Henry isn't as strange as you think. It's a fact I don't know what is going to happen between us in the long term—'

'And while you both make your minds up,' Xavier said scathingly, 'he allows you to travel to Peru and spend all your time with another man.' He made a typically Latin sound of contempt—a sound that, in spite of everything, brought a wry smile to Sophie's lips.

'How can you smile?' Xavier demanded incredulously. 'Henry might permit this—'

'Henry doesn't *permit* anything,' Sophie pointed out. 'I chart my own course—'

'On to the rocks?' Xavier demanded, embroidering his metaphor with some choice Spanish curses.

'I came to Peru to work as a doctor,' Sophie pointed out, 'in case you had forgotten. Why should Henry have any concerns? Forging a personal relationship with anyone here has never been on my agenda.'

'Well, that's great. I'm happy for you,' Xavier said sardonically, drawing to an abrupt halt so that they both jolted forward in their seats.

'Is this it?' Sophie said, apprehensively glancing about, wondering if she should get out.

'It's as far as I go,' Xavier said, resting his hands on the wheel as he turned to level a stare on her face.

Sophie felt there was more to his comment than simply an indication that their journey by truck had come to an end.

'Well?' he demanded impatiently. 'Are you going to get out? Or do you intend to sit there all day? And take something with you,' he added, making a curt gesture with his chin towards the bulging rucksacks in the back. Grabbing one, he swung out of the cab and started off without her in the direction of a natural stone staircase that Sophie guessed time and erosion had carved into the towering cliff a short distance from where they were parked.

'I'm still waiting for an apology,' she reminded him when she caught him up. The pack was heavy and unwieldy on her back, but she had no intention of showing the slightest sign of weakness—in any direction.

'An apology?' It was on the tip of his tongue to tell her where she could stick her apology, but when she looked at him like that, with the light of battle burning so strong in her eyes, all Xavier remembered was that the chase was back on. Under the circumstances, he could afford to be magnanimous. 'I'll agree to a truce,' he conceded. 'For now.'

'You're so gracious.'

'Aren't I?' he growled. 'Give me your pack, and I'll—'

'Thank you, I can manage,' Sophie said with determination.

Xavier headed off without so much as a glance over his shoulder to see if she was following him or not. Picking up speed, she managed to move ahead of him on the shallower part of the climb. But the rock face was far steeper than she had anticipated. Each foothold had to be chosen with care, and the pack was holding her back. She was soon forced to pause with her hands resting on her knees and watch him go past.

'Let me know if you need my help, won't you?' Xavier challenged sardonically before attacking the next challenge.

'Oh, don't worry, I will,' Sophie assured him as she caught her breath.

'Are you OK?' he said, peering down as he clung on to an overhanging ledge.

'I'm fine—thank you for asking.' And that rear view was spectacularly good, Sophie thought, admiring Xavier's tight, muscular frame. She was in no hurry to overtake him now.

'Are you going to join me? If it's too much for you—' He shrugged.

Sophie gasped. Xavier was lying flat on the ledge above her head, hanging over it, and their faces were almost touching. She had only lost concentration for a moment or two, but long enough for him to know she'd been staring at him.

'You're so arrogant!'

'And you love it,' he said confidently. 'Come,' he commanded. 'Take the pack off and let me lift it up here, then give me your hands.'

'You can't,' Sophie protested, looking behind her. They had already climbed up quite a way. If she fell...

'Don't you trust me, Sophie?'

Sending the rucksack up first, Sophie put her hands in Xavier's. He changed the grip, taking hold of her wrists instead, and seconds later she was standing next to him on the moss-covered ledge.

'First impressions?' he said, searching her eyes.

'First impressions?' Sophie muttered faintly.

'The view,' he said, grabbing her shoulders to turn her around. 'That's the only reason I can think of for bringing you here. So? What do you think of it?'

Sophie let herself relax just a little against him. The ledge overlooked the valley—no, the world, she thought, struggling to find the words to answer his question. The relics of one of the most dazzling of all South American civilisations was laid out before them, the intricate terracing a testament to the determination of its people to tame the land and thrive. 'It's spellbinding—timeless…'

He pulled her closer into him, and she realised how close to the edge they were.

'Not timeless for the Inca people,' he murmured, keeping his arms closer around her as he spoke. 'It took just a handful of conquistadores, with their armour, guns, horses and treachery, to destroy this highly developed civilisation in the span of a single generation.'

Sophie moved restlessly beneath the persuasive caress of his warm breath on a very sensitive part of her neck. It was so seductive, but some part of her warned he was only toying with her—testing her resolve. And, that apart, she sensed an anger behind his words that forced her to challenge the reason behind it. 'Surely you don't hold yourself responsible for that too?' She froze as his grip tightened around her shoulders, and when she turned she saw his eyes were flint-hard.

'Meaning, what exactly?'

'I don't know. I just sensed—'

'You sensed?' Xavier prompted.

He drew out the word as if it was both a blessing and a curse, which in many ways, to Sophie, it was. Facts she could handle. Coping with senses, emotions—that was much harder. But with Xavier it was different—she could sense things with him, Sophie realised, as if they were tuned to the same frequency and all she had to do was direct an unspoken question at him for it to be answered. She could feel the guilt lashing him when he mentioned the conquistadores, the same guilt he felt when Armando came into his mind. It made her want to reach out to him—physically, as well as emotionally. Their faces were almost touching. She was close enough to detect his warm, minty breath blending with the cool mountain air, and there were overtones of musky scent and warm, clean man…

'Sophie?' He made her concentrate on his face instead of staring dreamily into the middle distance. And when she managed to tear her gaze away, he got hold of her chin and brought her back again. 'You sensed what?' Xavier pressed. He felt her tense. She blew hot and cold—desire followed by panic. It was always the same. But why? Telling himself he was in danger of becoming too involved, Xavier hardened his heart to shut her out. If Sophie had a problem, his medical training was what he should draw on—not some false compassion that came from his impatience to bed her. 'Why don't you let me help you?' he said matter-of-factly. 'If you've got a problem, I'll help you get to the bottom of it—I'm a doctor, remember?'

Wrenching herself away from him so abruptly Xavier was forced to fling out an arm to stop her falling over the edge, Sophie exclaimed angrily, 'Don't give me that! You don't understand everything just because you're a doctor, Xavier!' She whipped her head away when he dragged her close again. 'You don't...you just don't, OK?'

'Perhaps I understand more than you think.' Frustration did strange things to people, Xavier mused. And if that was the only problem she had—once he was completely sure Henry was out of the picture he would sort it for her with the greatest of pleasure.

'No, no, you don't,' Sophie insisted weakly.

'I think I do,' Xavier husked gently, holding her in front of him and dipping his head so that their eyes were on a level.

'Could you help?' Sophie murmured.

'We can find the cure together,' he said wryly.

'How?' she whispered.

Xavier felt the soft brush of her breath on his lips. 'Like this maybe,' he suggested softly.

As their lips touched the world swam out of focus for Sophie and, when his tongue teased the seam of her mouth, her mind followed. All she was aware of was an intensity of sensation that filled every inch of her with pleasure. Xavier was so sure of himself it left no room for doubt. She trusted him completely…could relax into the love-play and, even though he was hardly touching her, she felt cocooned in a safe and sensual embrace from which she never wanted to escape. Using only his lips, tongue and the lightest pressure of his hands, Xavier showed her how lovemaking could be, driving away the savage memories that lurked deep in her mind. He drew out the sensual pleasures to their fullest extent so that every one of his drugging, beguiling kisses spoke of the next phase being even more to her liking.

'So, Sophie,' he murmured at last, his lips so close Sophie felt hers tingle in response, 'would you like me to undertake the treatment of this problem for you?'

She searched his eyes for signs of derision or contempt, but all she could detect was a degree of humour and affection that warmed her to the core. 'Only if it doesn't hurt,' she said wryly, risking a smile.

'It may sting a little at first,' Xavier admitted, raising his shoulders in a small shrug, 'but—' As his fingers meshed in her hair, cupping her head to gently bring her back for more kisses, Sophie sucked in a soft breath.

'Relax, *querida*, I'm not going to hurt you.'

As he nuzzled his face against her neck, Sophie gasped with pleasure and slipped her hands around his waist. He felt warm…wonderful. Her eyelids fluttered closed as she let her fingertips tell her all she needed to know, exploring further, moving upwards, growing bolder, until she was learning about every inch of his powerful, muscular back.

'Still afraid?' Xavier demanded, whispering into her ear.

Yes. But only because a dam of feelings was about to burst, and she didn't know if she would be able to control them. 'No,' Sophie whispered. And, as far as the debilitating panic was concerned, for the first time in her life she really meant it.

'Good,' Xavier murmured with a slow, curving smile. Their lips were almost touching again, but he pulled back a little to read her eyes…and then he allowed their lips to touch, but barely. And now, when Xavier deepened the kiss, Sophie moulded into him until she thought she would drown in sensation.

He tasted of fresh berries, good wine, and fruit gums, and of everything she had ever enjoyed in her life…and, as his kisses became more heated, deeper and more demanding, instead of pulling away from him, she moved closer.

'You're not frightened of me any longer,' he observed in a low voice, looking searchingly into her eyes as he caressed her face with one strong, tanned hand.

Frightened of him? All Sophie knew at this moment was a longing for him to possess her totally. It was so deep, so profound, she could think of nothing else. She needed more, so much more than a kiss.

'I'm not frightened of you,' she said honestly. He was the only teacher she needed—wanted. She knew now that only Xavier held the key to all the passion lying dormant inside her. But, instead of dragging her down with him on to the soft, mossy ground as she had expected and hoped, his eyes narrowed thoughtfully.

'And Henry is out of your life?' he said softly.

Sophie swallowed as the heat rushed to her cheeks. Henry was the very last subject she wanted to discuss.

'I could never entertain a relationship that wasn't completely exclusive,' Xavier murmured, dropping kisses on her neck.

She didn't doubt him for a minute.

Cupping her chin in his hand so she couldn't avoid his eyes, he said steadily, 'You do know that I mean that, don't you, Sophie?'

Before she had the chance to answer, they both heard the shout.

'Ah, here come our couriers,' Xavier murmured with satisfaction.

Sophie pulled away self-consciously. She had grown increasingly receptive until her nipples were hard and outthrust against the spread of his chest. Nothing like this had ever happened to her before—even her lips were swollen in a very visible sign that she was aroused. As two men appeared, cresting a rise to one side of them, she forced what had happened out of her mind. It was too raw, too revealing, to share with anyone, let alone strangers.

The exchange of introductions and rucksacks was undertaken rapidly and, the moment the two Peruvian health workers had left, Xavier turned back to her.

'I hope we may have something worth progressing when you have convinced me that Henry is not, and never will be, a part of your life,' he said coolly, as if the interlude when normality briefly intervened had never occurred.

Sophie searched his eyes angrily. They were cool and uncompromising. But how could he refer to what had just happened between them as *something worth progressing*?

'Shall we go?' he said, before she had the chance to marshal her thoughts.

Nodding her head briefly, Sophie followed him to the truck. She didn't trust herself to speak right now—not with Xavier's ultimatum still ringing in her ears.

By the time they got back the yard was full of people again, but not patients. There was a fiercely competitive football match going on between members of the medical staff and some of the boys from the village. The dusty space in front of the clinic had been transformed, and a blaze of excitement rose from the local supporters.

As Xavier drove in slowly through the gates he had to steer cautiously through the crowds of people milling about. 'Looks like fun,' he commented, resting his arms on the steering wheel to peer through the windscreen.

It was the first time he had spoken since mentioning *something worth progressing*! Sophie had tried to put it out of her mind and found she couldn't. But Xavier had probably been embarking on *something worth progressing* since the day he first had to shave. 'Will you drop me off here?' she demanded edgily.

'Let me park up first,' he said, 'and then I'll join you.'

Sophie flung her brightly coloured shawl around her shoulders in defiance. She felt like telling him not to bother. But the shiver of anticipation, the ice between her shoulder blades, told her he was behind her the moment she climbed out of the truck.

The first person she saw amongst the crowd was Anna Groes. It must be a day for self-flagellation, Sophie mused, as she hurried towards the Danish doctor.

'Hey, Xavier, come and help us—we're being destroyed here.'

The voice of the man jogging backwards alongside her told Sophie Xavier was close. She didn't need telling. She was caught up in his powerful aura; she could feel it spinning a silken web all around her—electrifying, stimulating—it quite literally took her breath away.

'Will you be OK if I leave you?'

She turned. Xavier's expression was sardonic. He was all male. He loved the chase. 'I'll be fine.' Sophie's heart thundered a warning. Her pulse hammered a tattoo. Then, out of the corner of her eye, she spotted the family who had given her the beautiful shawl. She was so relieved she exclaimed out loud and stood on tiptoe to wave to them. But a curl of apprehension wormed its way down Sophie's spine as she made her break for freedom and, when she turned around, she found Anna Groes watching her.

Banishing Anna from her thoughts, and doing the best she could to do the same for Xavier, Sophie concentrated on getting to know the family. She completely lost track of time until the game ended and Xavier led his team to victory.

'I'd better go,' she said and, as the family waved her off, she hurried back through the crowd, using Anna's sleek blonde head as a guide.

'I'm sorry, I didn't mean to leave you on your own.'

'I was OK,' Anna said impatiently. 'And I imagine you were glad of the break. Don't you find Xavier exhausting?'

'Exhausting?' Sophie said, then she remembered the climb to the ledge and the swimming. 'He is very fit.'

'Very fit,' Anna agreed sardonically. 'There aren't many women who can keep up with him. I congratulate you.'

This was not a pat on the back, Sophie sensed, finding it troubling. As they entered the clinic Xavier emerged from the shower.

Whatever their differences, it didn't stop Sophie's whole being ache at the sight of him. There was a towel slung around his bronzed neck, and his low-slung jeans moulded his powerful thighs, while the black fitted top clung to his imposing frame—he hadn't even dried himself properly, she noted wryly, seeing some drops of water tracking down his neck. He was certainly in a hurry to get somewhere…he was certainly irresistible too, she mused, pinning a casual expression to her face.

'Xavier! You were wonderful!' Anna effused, throwing her arms around his neck. She would have kissed him square on the lips, had he not turned round to look at Sophie as she struck.

'Sorry to disillusion you, but I'm not the hero of the hour,' Xavier said coolly. 'I didn't arrange the match.'

'But you saved the day by scoring the winning goal,' Anna pointed out with a pout.

Raking the towel back and forth across his neck, Xavier made a dismissive sound.

'Why don't I make us something to eat?' Anna purred, still gazing at him.

He looked thoughtful. 'Perhaps we should give each other a little space. After all, we work together all day.'

His glance embraced Sophie, and it hurt. 'I was hoping to discuss work schedules with you over supper, Xavier,' she pointed out. 'I don't mind helping you to prepare the meal, Anna—'

'That's very good of you, Sophie,' Xavier said dryly, 'but I've got something else in mind.'

Sophie felt let down and furious. Xavier couldn't just cut

her out of the working loop because he was too busy. Or was he punishing her because of his suspicions about Henry?

'I've got a prior invitation,' he said with a shrug when she threw him a look.

'Fine,' Sophie countered. 'I take it you'll be posting a roster on the board so that I can see what's expected of me?'

'I'll let you know what's expected of you.'

'I can tell Sophie,' Anna offered, suddenly helpful, 'over supper.'

'I'm sorry, Anna,' Xavier said, turning to look at her, 'but Sophie's coming with me.'

'With you?'

The two women's voices chimed as one as they gazed at Xavier in surprise.

'Where?' Sophie demanded, as her heart began to race.

'To make a visit.'

'A medical visit?'

'It is connected with my medical interests,' Xavier volunteered.

'Why didn't you tell me about this before?'

'It must have slipped my mind.'

His shrug was mildly apologetic, but he didn't look a bit sorry, Sophie decided. She jumped as the sound of Anna's door slamming reached them.

'Well, are you ready?' Xavier said, tossing the towel which had been slung around his neck on to a chair. 'Grab a jacket; it gets cold quickly.'

And, before she could ask any more questions, he strode past her out of the door.

Xavier could feel his senses simmering as he settled himself behind the wheel. He had never had to wait for anything in his life before—and what was the truth about Henry Whitland? A fierce sound shot from his throat as he remembered. *He would not share her.*

He made a low sound of satisfaction, remembering

Sophie's arousal when he held her in his arms. He had developed a taste for her sweetness, and had begun the cure—but, if she wanted the full treatment, she had some urgent decisions to make.

CHAPTER SIX

'SO WHERE are we really going?' Sophie said.

'I want you to see the type of direction our work must take for this project to be successful in the long term,' Xavier told her. 'Don't worry, we'll get something to eat.'

'I'm not worried about food,' Sophie said honestly. She was more concerned in the shift in his mood, because for once she couldn't read it. 'Can we talk about the rota?' she said innocently, searching his face for clues.

'If we must.'

She tried another tack. 'You said we had an invitation?'

'Why don't you just wait and see?' Xavier said, spinning the wheel as he drove out of the compound.

'Xavier, I—'

'What?'

'I need to get something straight with you.' When he remained silent she went straight on. 'Henry—'

His snort of derision cut her off.

'I'm going to tell you about Henry,' Sophie insisted. 'Whether or not you want to hear, you're going to hear this.'

Xavier's jaw was ground tight as he leaned over to turn the radio on.

'This is important, Xavier,' Sophie warned, turning it off again.

'OK, so I'm listening,' he said tersely.

Taking a deep, steadying breath, Sophie said bluntly, 'I'm not engaged to Henry. I never have been engaged to Henry. We've known each other for years. The ring was a token of the friendship between us. That's it.' She waited for him to say something but, apart from a slight movement of his head, accompanied by a similar acknowledgement from his lips, he had no comment to make.

Well, she'd done it, Sophie reflected. What else could she say?

Xavier had difficulty keeping his mouth shut—had difficulty stopping himself from ramming the brakes on and seducing her in the truck. It wasn't quite what he'd hoped for, but what the hell? The gear lever might get in the way, but he could kneel on the floor and there was a ledge under the windscreen to rest her feet on... Was he going completely loco? Probably, Xavier answered himself dryly. Sophie had told him exactly what he had wanted to hear—he just hadn't anticipated hearing it quite so soon.

'Are we coming to another village?' Sophie said, breaking into his thoughts.

'That's right,' Xavier said, pulling himself round with difficulty. 'You must be hungry.'

His consideration was a straw suggesting they could remain civil with each other and Sophie grabbed at it. 'I am,' she agreed with a smile in her voice.

Xavier drew up in front of one of the many rough stone dwellings, and Sophie saw that the wooden entrance door was pushed a small way open. A soft glow of light came from the inside. 'A café?' she guessed.

'My friend's home,' Xavier explained, as he reached over the seat into the space behind.

Sophie hadn't noticed the bulging bag before, and Xavier offered no explanation as he threw the strap over his shoulder and climbed down from the truck.

As they went into the modest home together the warmth of the family's welcome enveloped Sophie immediately. Escorting her to a comfortably padded bench at one side of the fire blazing brightly in the tiled hearth, they clustered around her like brightly plumaged birds concerned for their long-lost chick. The air was filled with the tang of wood smoke, overlaid with the aroma of something good cooking, and everywhere Sophie looked there were colourful examples of the local pottery, as well as the fabulous woven textiles everyone took for granted in Peru.

Xavier introduced her to Agustin and Francisca. Their six children ranged in age from a babe in arms to a serious-faced boy called Marcos, who Sophie judged to be around seventeen. The whole family was openly delighted by their visit, but Marcos especially seemed thrilled to see Xavier.

One of the older girls poured Sophie a drink from the pitcher standing on the wooden table, whilst another brought over a platter of fruit and cheese for her to pick at. Smiling her thanks, Sophie wondered if their distinctive dress was unique to that village. Rather than the usual jaunty fedoras, their heads were covered with a warm, heat-retaining fabric, similar to felt, with a heavy fringe around the edges, so that it resembled a soft and rather flattering lampshade. The girl with the cheekiest grin had decorated hers with a splash of vivid embroidery—personalised it, like teenagers everywhere, Sophie thought, smiling up at her. All the female members of the family wore colourful shawls similar to her own over red cardigans or jumpers, and their skirts were full, in dark grey edged with bands of red.

'There's soup,' the father, Agustin, said with a kindly smile, 'with vegetables I grew myself. I hope you will join us.'

'I'd love to,' Sophie said. 'Your English is very good. I'm afraid I only speak the little Spanish I picked up on holiday in my childhood.'

'But you are a doctor,' he said gently, as if this was a place where no one fell short in any way. 'And I work in the tourist industry,' he went on to explain, as if his command of a second language was nothing special. 'I work at—'

'Rancho del Condor?' Sophie guessed.

'That's right,' he answered with obvious pleasure.

Sophie could feel Xavier watching her. Glancing up, she found she was right. He was pleased by her interest; she could see it in his eyes. She dragged her gaze away from him to listen as Agustin continued. 'My wife, Francisca, speaks English too, and the children will learn,' he stated firmly, as if that was a direct instruction to all of them.

Smiling back at Agustin and looking around at his family, Sophie felt the same tug in her heart she guessed Xavier felt whenever he came here.

She glanced over to where Xavier was sitting with the older boy, and was surprised when he looked up. There was something raw in his stare that commanded her attention, but then he too turned back to listen to whatever Marcos was saying to him. They were seated together in an area arranged for privacy. A colourful swag of the typical, mostly red Peruvian cloth was strung between two poles in one corner of the room, and their stools were pulled so close together that their heads were almost touching. And now she knew the secret of the bulging bag—medical books.

'Well, I don't need them,' Xavier said with a dismissive gesture, when she asked him about it later on the way home.

'So, Marcos—'

'Wants to be a doctor,' Xavier said, anticipating her question.

'But how—?'

'There's a scholarship.' He left it at that.

'The Armando Martinez Bordiu Scholarship?' Sophie said gently.

'That's right,' he said.

When the lights of the clinic came into sight Xavier slowed the truck before they got there and, finding a clearing at one side of the road, he pulled in and cut the engine.

'Where are we now?' Sophie asked curiously.

'Somewhere,' he said, turning to look at her. 'Does it matter?'

Sophie's heart had picked up pace until she could hardly breathe. 'Of course not, I just wondered.'

Leaning across the seat, Xavier began toying with the soft fringe that, as usual, had tumbled into her eyes.

Automatically reaching up to push it away, Sophie's fingers encountered his. Moving of their own accord, or so it seemed to her, they twined through his and rested there for a while. Just having their hands locked together was enough to make her breathing ragged. It sounded loud in the silence of the darkened cab. Raising the game, Xavier began caressing her palm with a sensitive, compelling touch, and then he moved on to stroke the blue-white veins showing her raised pulse clearly beneath her fine, sun-blushed skin.

'So, why are we here?' Sophie managed in a voice that sounded faint against the heartbeat thundering in her ears.

'Because I'm not ready to go back yet,' Xavier said, steering a glance at her.

'But why—?'

'Has anyone ever told you that you ask too many questions?'

'Yes,' Sophie admitted softly, 'you.'

'Well, you haven't changed a bit since the day I first met you, Sophie Ford. You still ask far too many questions.'

His voice was low, little more than a whisper. Sophie felt her level of awareness soar to match his.

'Are you seriously telling me you have never done this before?' Xavier demanded softly.

'Done what?'

His answer was a kiss. His mouth barely touched hers. He held himself back deliberately, knowing the moment he stopped kissing her she would want more.

'Kissed in the back of a car,' Xavier continued, teasing her mercilessly with the lightest brush of his lips on her face, her neck, her eyelids, 'or the front of a truck, in this case,' he murmured, his quiet laughter mingling with her sighs as Sophie swayed towards him, groaning in need. 'What is it, *querida*? Do you want this?' he murmured, returning to tease the seam of her lips with his tongue.

Sophie could only shudder out a sigh, but she was trembling with sensation when he moved away again, this time to drop kisses along the line of her jaw.

'Or this?' he suggested softly. Having reached the lobe of

her ear, he took it delicately between his lips to suckle, the heat of his breath causing every fine hair on her neck to stand erect. His kisses on the nape of her neck made her move languorously on the seat. She seemed to have lost all semblance of control over her body, and could only writhe in anticipation when his searing glance challenged her to deny the extent of her arousal.

'Or this—'

She cried out as his powerful hand enclosed the soft swell of her breast, and in the next moment she was pressing against him, not caring what he might think of her, linking her hands behind his neck, dragging him to her, seeking his mouth and kissing him hard, opening her lips beneath his, inviting his possession, relishing the erotic clash of his tongue against her own. She didn't want any more talk, any more teasing… She wanted the touch of his hand nursing her breast to last for ever. She loved the fact that he found her nipple unhesitatingly through her clothes and that he knew just how to touch her, how to make her find extremes of pleasure she had never known existed. She was greedy, she had been starved of physical love too long and, ripping her shirt open, she seized his other hand and made him claim her neglected breast, folding her own hand around his to increase the pressure and leave him in no doubt that this was what she needed.

'Or is this what you really want?' he murmured, easing her thighs apart.

Sophie gasped. Even through the fabric of her summer-weight jeans she was sure they could both feel the heat and, in the slanting shafts of moonshine streaming into the cab, see the swollen signs of her arousal. But, as her hands rushed to the top button above the zip, Xavier stopped her, and firmly moved them away.

'Not yet,' he warned softly. 'We've a long way to go before we get that far.'

'What do you mean?' Sophie groaned breathlessly, writhing a little beneath his firm touch. 'I want… I need—'

'I know,' Xavier said soothingly. 'I know exactly what you need.' And then one of his hands was between her legs, and his long, lean fingers began stroking—lightly, rhythmically so that Sophie could only issue little surprised cries of pleasure and relief.

He brought her to the edge with unhurried ease, and when he tipped her over the small cab echoed with her cries and then with her whimpers of exhaustion and delight as the violent waves of pleasure subsided gradually into eddies of contentment.

'Now do you trust me to know what you need?' Xavier murmured as he drew her back into his arms.

Sophie sighed raggedly against his lips as she parted her swollen lips for more of his kisses. She wanted more, she wanted everything he could give her—everything he could teach her. It was like a dam bursting inside her, or waking up after a long sleep. Xavier had shown her reserves of desire she could never have guessed she possessed. And when he kissed her this time they met on equal ground, Sophie welcoming the thought-robbing passion that left nothing but sensation, nothing but Xavier. She sighed with contentment as he brought her deeper into the circle of his arms, pulling open his jacket to draw her inside.

'Better, *querida*?' he asked softly, nuzzling his face against her neck.

'Much, much better.'

'Are you warm enough?'

Beautifully, thrillingly, completely. 'Yes, really, really warm,' Sophie confirmed softly.

'Good,' Xavier murmured, smiling against her lips.

His kisses were tender and compelling now, like a dance of delight she never wanted to end. Sophie could not have given herself more willingly as she moulded against him, all pliant and eager, like a fresh green shoot setting out on its first journey towards the sun. And when at last he pulled away she felt bereft, lost, and wondered how she could bear a single moment of parting from him.

'Don't look so worried,' Xavier said, straightening up to switch on the engine. 'We've got clinic tomorrow, remember? It's been a very long day, but a good one, and now we should get some sleep.'

'Xavier...'

'Yes?'

'Can I ask you something?'

His expression suggested they had few secrets from each other now. But Sophie wasn't so sure.

'What is it?'

'Anna Groes.'

He turned off the engine and swung round in his seat to face her. 'What about Anna Groes?'

'That's what I need to know,' Sophie admitted, dreading what had to come next, but knowing that she had to go ahead now she'd started. 'What does she mean to you?'

'Nothing,' he admitted flatly. 'She means nothing to me.'

'But once—'

'We were lovers,' he said casually, as if it was an everyday occurrence to use and discard someone like a carton of milk.

Sophie felt as if she was contracting in on herself—as if the whole world was pressing her down, making her smaller and smaller like Alice until at last she would disappear.

'Like your *open* relationship with Henry,' Xavier said with a shrug, as if that was explanation enough. 'We're adults, we have needs,' he concluded dismissively, firing the engine again.

So that was what Anna meant by *keeping up with* Xavier, Sophie thought as he let in the clutch and the truck began to move. It was almost funny. Or might have been if she hadn't fallen in love with him... Pressing her lips together as she contemplated the truth behind the sudden rogue thought, Sophie turned to stare blindly out of the window. Yes, she had fallen in love. Pathetic really, wasn't it—when Xavier was only in lust. Here she was looking for a lifetime's commitment while he wanted nothing more than a sexual interlude to satisfy his *needs*. And the bottom line? If she couldn't have Xavier on her terms, would she take him on his?

Yes.

After slipping the rest of her photos from home around the frame of the mirror, and draping the beautiful scarf she had been given over a shelf where she could admire it, Sophie lay awake, staring into the darkness. Xavier knew how to play her senses until she was screaming for release. But he had been firm about sleeping alone, so now she had only her thoughts to keep her company. Thinking of him, lying asleep so close with only a thin partition separating them, Sophie reached out a hand from under the covers and rested her palm noiselessly against the cool, smooth surface as if she could draw some of his essence through the divide and somehow be soothed by it. She couldn't sleep, not for one moment. Everything was in turmoil. Xavier wanted her. She wanted him. It should have been simple, but what was? If life had been simple they would be in bed together right now.

She had never wanted a man in such an overwhelming and totally consuming way. She wanted him completely: every nuance in his character, good and bad; each glint in his eye; all the smiles, all the laughter, and all his sorrow too.

She wanted his body. And she wanted it now.

Sophie shifted position restlessly, but nothing gave her comfort. Nothing could—nothing but Xavier by her side, naked and demanding. But he had made it plain that he would not be hurried. Any relationship between them would be strictly short-term, and it would start when he was ready, or not at all.

She turned towards the window. Someone was trying to attract her attention. Dragging back one of the coarse, raw blue curtains, she peered out into the darkness. Agustin beckoned to her. Grabbing the rest of her clothes, Sophie quickly pulled them on. Carrying her shoes, she sneaked silently past Xavier's room and went outside to see what was wrong.

Agustin struggled to remain calm as he explained that he

had left his van parked some way from the clinic in order not to disturb everyone. Then Sophie learned she was sleeping in Xavier's old room, hence Agustin's mistake when he tapped on her window.

'Should we wake him?' Agustin said uncertainly.

'No, no, he has early clinic tomorrow. I'll come with you,' Sophie said. The problem sounded like something she knew a lot about; something she could handle alone—and the village wasn't that far away.

It took just a few minutes to collect everything she needed and soon they were speeding down the road in Agustin's van. They were almost at the outskirts of the village when the van jerked several times, slowed, and finally stopped. With a huff of frustration, Agustin banged his hands on the wheel.

'Never mind,' Sophie said, covering his hand with her own. 'We can walk from here,' she pointed out, quickly gathering her bags.

'I'm so sorry about this!' Agustin exclaimed as he swung one of her bags on to his own shoulder.

'It's fine, don't worry about it. You were right to come and get me,' Sophie said reassuringly.

It didn't take them long to cover the rest of the distance. Flickering lights were already beginning to show in some of the houses as slumbering fires were coaxed into life to ward off the chill of the dawn. Agustin's was no exception. Following him inside, Sophie found one of his daughters lying on a makeshift settle by the fire, alternately coughing and struggling to breathe. Marcos was holding her up in his arms, but when he saw Sophie he looked relieved and then, realising Xavier wasn't with her, his expression became anxious again.

It didn't take Sophie long to conclude that her first thoughts had been correct. Opening her medical bag, she reached inside for her stethoscope and all the other paraphernalia she would need to confirm her diagnosis. The constriction in the young girl's chest, the build up of mucus, the distinctive wheezing, confirmed her initial thoughts. Sophie was sure she was dealing with an asthma attack. Fortunately, before she had left the clinic, Agustin had briefed her well enough for her to anticipate everything she would need.

With the family's help she pulled the settle away from the fire and made sure the girl was propped up on cushions. After administering an injection, she raised a saline drip and showed the family how to use the portable nebuliser she had brought with her. This delivered medication in a fine mist, allowing it to be absorbed quickly and efficiently. Once the face mask was in place the sounds of hectic breathing eased quickly and the blue tinge around the young girl's mouth and the base of her fingernails disappeared. But, even with this level of improvement, Sophie was concerned that she should be admitted to hospital for observation as soon as possible.

Agustin assured her that this would be done as soon as he had asked one of his friends to take them there. 'The Armando Martinez Bordiu Hospital is good, very good,' he said confidently. 'Our health care is excellent since Dr Xavier came here to us. He pays for everything.'

Smiling reassuringly, Sophie was relieved to see that her patient was already able to sit up and talk to her brothers and sisters, inhaling oxygen through a mask from the small portable tank she had brought with her.

As she sat down to write a report for the hospital, the unaffected happiness of the family struck a chord deep inside her. She envied them, she realised—envied the unconditional love she felt around her.

For some reason Xavier forced his way into her mind. What a joke, Sophie mused, telling herself to dismiss that fantasy right away. Something like this was never going to happen for her with Xavier. To him she was just a potential conquest. A woman no one had succeeded in awakening—what man could resist a challenge like that? It didn't make her special to him, it just appealed to his masculine pride—even perhaps to his scientific mind as a doctor. She was, after all, something of a curiosity as far as sex was concerned.

Suddenly the need to be on her own for a while overcame

everything, even caution, and, picking up her bags, Sophie slipped out of the door without anyone noticing.

She hadn't realised the village was quite so far away from the clinic, and the return journey seemed never-ending now that she was on foot and alone. She kept up a brisk pace, occasionally breaking into a jog when she couldn't identify the noises in the undergrowth, and tried not to let her imagination run away with her. But there were places where the road narrowed and the canopy of trees closed across it so that the thin morning sunbeams came in grudging threads through a dense tunnel of leaves.

She was scared and tired, and had lost track of how much further she had to go. The first clearing she came to, she picked out a tree standing closest to the road and sat down, leaning her back against the rough surface of its trunk, intending just to rest for a few minutes.

The sound of a truck being driven at high speed jolted her alert with a start. And when she saw it was Xavier driving, she stumbled to her feet and began shouting and waving with relief.

'Sophie!' Leaping down from the truck, he grabbed her by the shoulders in an iron grip, his eyes scouring her face for signs of harm. 'Thank God you're all right!'

But as Sophie slumped with relief he challenged her angrily, 'What the hell do you think you're doing out here all alone?'

'I was only resting for a moment.'

'Resting?' he grated incredulously. He turned away from her to rake stiff fingers through his hair, and then turned back again. 'Where the hell do you think you are, Surrey?'

Suddenly it was all too much for her—Xavier towering over her, blotting out the sun, confirming the chasm she knew existed between her fantasies and the reality of the situation between them. 'Go away!' Sophie exploded furiously. 'Get back in your damn truck! Just leave me alone!'

'I'll do no such thing!' He caught hold of her and dragged her back. 'I'm not leaving you here. You're coming back with me, Sophie. For God's sake, woman! I know what you've done!'

His voice was raw and harsh, and Sophie gasped when he brought her close and held her tight against him.

'Agustin called me from the hospital,' he said fiercely against her hair. 'He told me what happened. He was frantic with worry.' Xavier took a moment to calm himself. 'You did great, but that doesn't mean you should ever repeat this—' He gestured around fiercely, an expression of complete incomprehension darkening his face, and when words finally failed him he just hissed with frustration. 'Next time, just wake me, OK?' Xavier rode over her attempt to apologise. 'You could have had an accident, Sophie! Don't you understand? When you act on impulse, people get hurt—'

There was a subtle shift in his voice, enough to alert her. And when she looked into his eyes Sophie knew they were both thinking the same thing—and it had nothing to do with her reckless journey back from the village. It concerned a wicked dare made by her own drunken father, a set of keys to a high-performance car, and Xavier's fatally impulsive kid brother.

She gasped when he dragged her close with a sudden explosion of passion. But even cloaked in his strength Sophie knew, however many ghosts she lived with, Xavier had his own—and they could drive them apart just as surely as they had brought them together.

It was a relentless game that would never end until they both faced up to what had happened years back and found closure. But until all the ghosts were banished and Xavier could talk about his brother, there was no comfort she could offer him, other than the temporary warmth and reassurance of an embrace.

CHAPTER SEVEN

ON A scale of one to ten, Sophie's stress levels over the next few days went off the chart. Everything that had happened had encouraged her to believe that Xavier's special brand of therapy would continue...that they might grow closer. But when he kept his distance she was forced to remind herself yet again that he was just a great doctor—and they both had a job to do.

On the morning he made a general announcement at breakfast to say that he was returning to Lima on business, her feelings came to a boil. She had to say something. If he was leaving, then she had a right to know what her job entailed. And if it bounced him into some sort of action on the personal front...

'It won't disrupt the rota,' Xavier said, sweeping the room with his dark glance—a glance that simply included Sophie in with the rest of his colleagues.

Sophie reddened, knowing she had made a huge miscalculation. She wanted Xavier in every way; he wanted her services as a doctor—there was a world of difference between the two.

Determined not to dwell on it, she attacked the filing. So what if Xavier hadn't mentioned the trip to her beforehand? She wasn't about to trail after him everywhere he went, was she? She had her own job to do, and she—

'Filing?'

Sophie looked up, her eyes flashing warnings, her lips still pressed in a tight, angry line.

'Why?' Xavier demanded in a voice full of perfectly targeted challenge.

Slamming the drawer shut, Sophie straightened up to confront him. 'Because it needed doing.'

'Lola can handle it.'

'And so can I.'

Closing himself off to her had proved a waste of energy. So he'd throw this idea up in the air and wait to see where it landed, Xavier mused, riding over her testiness in a meltingly dark voice full of reason. 'But I saw you have a free morning and thought you might like to go for a swim.'

'Swim?'

'You seemed to enjoy yourself the last time we went swimming, and you look like you could do with cooling off,' he observed dryly.

'Can't you see I'm busy?' She saw the look of triumph on his face as Lola walked in. As Sophie smiled a welcome at her she knew she was trespassing on Lola's domain...knew when she was beaten too.

'Swim?' Xavier suggested with a touch more irony.

'A swim would be great,' Sophie agreed dryly.

'You take that man up to the lake and have some fun,' Lola advised, appearing to miss the undercurrents between them.

'Why don't I join you?'

They all wheeled round at the same time.

'Yes, why don't you?' Sophie effused, seeing Anna. 'That would be great, wouldn't it, Xavier?' At least she had the small satisfaction of seeing the glow of victory in his eyes stall.

'Can we just go?' he demanded impatiently.

'I'll get my things,' Sophie said obligingly. It just couldn't get any better, could it? But at least someone was happy about the situation, she mused wryly, glancing at Anna.

At the lake, Sophie pulled off her clothes to reveal the beautiful swimming costume in a shade so similar to her eyes that Xavier had picked out for her at the Rancho del Condor boutique. He was wearing the same swimming shorts as before, she noticed, relishing the sight of his naked back as he stripped off his top.

'Look at you two,' a shrill voice taunted from somewhere over her head. 'Grandma and grandpa, I presume?'

Shielding her eyes with her hand to fend off the rays of the sun, Sophie gazed up.

Completely naked, Anna stood poised on top of an over-hanging ledge surveying them both—and holding her stomach in for all she was worth, Sophie thought, allowing herself an extremely gratifying moment of bitchery.

'Xavier!' Anna called, clearly not going to be satisfied until she had captured his attention too. 'Race you to the other side?'

His answer was to dive in, and there was scarcely anything to show for his entry into the pool, Sophie saw, other than the series of circular ripples spreading slowly outwards. Like the thoughts in her own head, she realised, glancing at Anna. She was trying not to let her imagination run away with her, but it was difficult not to when Anna's whole attention was so blatantly focused on Xavier.

'Sorry, Anna,' Xavier called as he resurfaced and shook his head to clear the water from his face. 'This is purely relaxation for me. No races...no nothing.' He proved the point by turning over to float on his back in silence, with only the slightest movement of his hands to steer him and keep him afloat.

Had he noted the prominent breasts, nipples outthrust...or the fact that Anna wasn't a natural blonde, though she was certainly creative with a razor? If he had, Sophie decided, with a small smile, he was keeping his opinions to himself.

'Coming in, Sophie?' he drawled lazily, his voice carrying easily over the limpid water with its sounding boards of sheer, smooth-faced rock.

There was only one way to join him, and that was fast, Sophie thought, remembering how cold the water could be in the mountains. Stopping to think about it was just not an option!

When she reached his side, Xavier reached out and pulled her close. 'Race *you* to the bank?' he suggested in a low, teasing voice.

It was the first hint of intimacy between them since he'd stopped at the side of the road—and she was still feeling the effects of that, Sophie realised, as warmth flooded through her on cue.

'Fine, Mister,' she challenged. 'Any time you like.'

'Ten-second start?'

This time a look was enough to tell him what she thought of that. Launching herself into the race, Sophie pulled out all the stops and arrived on the opposite bank only a few seconds after Xavier.

Helping her to climb out, he reached for their towels and tossed one over to her.

Predictably, Anna was sunbathing in the nude.

'I'll go back in to swim again if you want company,' Sophie offered, towelling her hair vigorously.

'And get blue with cold? No thank you,' Anna drawled without opening her eyes. 'I'll just improve my tan,' she said, turning over to reveal a back view almost as impressive as the front.

Xavier seemed gratifyingly unimpressed, Sophie noticed as he moved into the shadows to dress.

But the fact that he seemed neither to notice nor to care what Anna was doing was not lost on the beautiful Dane. The look she lavished on Sophie was hard, and lasted a beat too long.

A challenge? Sophie wondered, feeling a prescient chill run through her.

Thankfully, on their return to the clinic the tension between everyone smoothed out. In fact, Anna dogged Sophie's footsteps, as if suddenly she was the most desirable company in the world. And, just when Sophie was beginning to wonder if the swimming trip had been just that—a swimming trip, Xavier came to find her.

'I thought I should warn you—'

'Warn me?' Sophie tensed, acutely aware of Anna standing right next to her.

'I know it's short notice,' he said, 'but you'll have to come with me tomorrow.'

'I will?' Sophie said, swallowing back her euphoria and attempting nonchalance.

'I could take the time off,' Anna offered, moving in front of Sophie to claim all Xavier's attention. 'There are plenty here who could cover for me.'

'That's good of you, Anna,' he said, 'but I need to make sure I leave a good spread of specialisms here to cover both the clinic and the hospital. Sophie will—'

'What?' Anna demanded, affronted. 'What will Sophie do for you that I can't?'

'I was about to say that Sophie will go where she is needed most, as you will, Anna,' Xavier said, in a voice that didn't invite contradiction.

'Of course,' she said, her face reddening as she backed down.

In that moment, Sophie had some sympathy for her fellow doctor. Who knew better than she how Xavier could invade your thoughts to the exclusion of everything else? And, in spite of everything, Anna was an excellent physician with a highly developed sense of responsibility towards her patients.

'Don't look so shocked,' Xavier murmured in Sophie's ear as he steered her in front of him and out through the door. 'You signed up to do anything that's required of you, remember?'

'So what's required of me?' she challenged, turning to confront him at the top of the steps.

'This,' he said, slamming the door shut with his foot and leaning back on it so it couldn't be opened from the inside.

As he dragged Sophie against him and dipped his head to kiss her, it was so unexpected she let out a soft cry before melting against him. His kiss was everything she had hoped for—hungry, tender, deep and long. He kissed her as if he had waited all his life for it, and he only let her go when it became obvious that someone—Anna, almost certainly, was trying to open the door from the other side.

'I don't like waiting,' Xavier growled fiercely against Sophie's lips, 'and I certainly didn't expect to wait so long for that.'

Before she could reply he had hold of her hand and was tugging her down the steps after him.

The sensation that she was a naughty child running away from the schoolmistress swept over Sophie as they ran to the truck. She didn't need to look behind her to know that Anna was standing beside the open door watching them.

'Where are we going?' Sophie said, catching her breath as Xavier hammered the engine on his way out of the compound.

'Where would you like to go?'

'Away from here?' she said lightly, searching his face for answers. 'So, Xavier, which is it, work or pleasure?'

'We'll save the work for tomorrow.'

'And today?' Sophie demanded softly. 'Where are we going, Xavier?'

'Somewhere where we can be alone—unless you've got any better ideas?'

'None,' Sophie said quickly. His voice was enough to seduce her without the need for anything else, she realised, basking in the persuasive heat toying with her senses.

'But I hope it's not too far away.' She received just the look she wanted from him—short, fierce, and knowing.

'My thoughts exactly,' Xavier agreed, increasing speed.

He drove up as far as the narrow track allowed, but then they had to get out and walk deeper into the closely packed trees until they came out again on to a ledge overlooking the valley. The silence was infinite, seclusion guaranteed, and from their incredible vantage point the plain below them seemed to stretch for ever in a patchwork of umber and sienna and soft, sunlit gold. Wherever rainwater had pooled, mosses and lichens flourished, providing acid green highlights. In the far distance the formidable Andes mountains rose in jagged crests, the menacing shade at their base offset by the timeless majesty of ice-blue fingers pointing towards infinity in a cloudless sapphire sky.

Sophie sank to the ground when Xavier drew her down with him, but when she expected him to kiss her again he only whispered, 'Stay very still.'

'What?' she murmured, searching his face.

'Over there…towards that peak,' he said, turning away from her to stare out intently across the plain, 'Do you see it?'

Following his gaze, Sophie sucked in a fast, surprised breath. Even at this distance she could tell the bird they were looking at was huge—no, massive. 'Is it a condor?' she demanded incredulously.

'Yes, it's a condor,' Xavier confirmed, whispering against her face. 'They come here to hunt in the late afternoon—and here comes his mate.' As he spoke he settled her on the comfortable mossy bed so that she was lying quite flat, and all the while his hand was steadily undoing her shirt. When his lips moved unerringly to the most sensitive part of her neck Sophie writhed sensuously beneath him, trying not to lose focus on the two colossal birds wheeling over their heads, performing a slow and graceful *pas de deux* for her alone—or so it seemed—wingtips touching, almost as if they were flirting. 'Xavier—'

'Yes?'

Sophie couldn't speak. He had the buttons undone and was moving down to lavish kisses on the soft swell of her breasts.

'What?' he whispered, tracing the outline of first one erect nipple and then the other beneath the fine lace of her bra with just the tantalisingly light touch of one thumbnail.

'You said it would be a long time before you—' Her voice faded into a sigh.

'Are you asking me to stop, Sophie?' Xavier murmured, his voice thick with desire as he watched her nipples firm still more beneath his touch.

'No, no, don't stop,' Sophie insisted breathlessly, meshing her fingers through his hair to bring him closer.

With a soft growl of triumph he moved again, this time to plunder the dark, moist recesses of her mouth with a purposeful rhythm, while his hands—his hands!

Moving suddenly, restlessly, Sophie sat up, slipped out of her shirt and tore off her bra. Freed from their lacy constraint she knew her breasts appeared large on her slender frame, and felt the sweet pain of nipples engorged, hard and tempting. She faced him and had the satisfaction of hearing Xavier's fast breath when he saw her naked from the waist up for the first time. She watched with savage pleasure as he took in the size of her breasts and saw the extent of her arousal. But still she held back. She wasn't finished with him yet—not by a long way. Not after all the torment he had put her through since that night in the truck. Maybe once she'd been compliant, but now she was impatient and needy—quarry turned aggressor. And when Xavier reached out to claim her, she denied him fiercely, bringing him to his knees as she turned her attentions to his clothing. Xavier responded instantly, removing her hands to tear at his shirt, and then tugging his close-fitting top over his head until they faced each other naked from the waist up, eyes burning with the fever of desire, lips parted to suck in the air they needed to fuel their passion. For a moment they paused, held immobile in a band of erotic tension. Sophie felt the power of her female heritage when she saw the fire in Xavier's eyes matched her own; they were a tableau of raw passion in a land of savage beauty.

'Come to me,' he commanded softly.

Getting to her feet, Sophie moved towards him, loosening the fastenings on her jeans slowly, provocatively; holding his glance, she stood a little in front of him while she steadily eased them down over her hips. Stepping out of them, she was about to do the same with the tiny thong she was wearing when he stopped her with a short, imperative wave of his hand. Making a small gesture, he encouraged her forward.

As he buried his head between her thighs and she felt his hot breath warming her, Sophie groaned and felt her legs weaken, but he would not let her down yet and held her firm to nuzzle his lips against her swollen flesh. He let her feel the gentle nip of his teeth against the damp swell of her arousal and teased her beyond bearing with his tongue through the cobweb of lace.

'Please, Xavier…please.'

'Not yet,' he warned, slipping his hand between her slim thighs to continue the work of his tongue.

As his fingers found her she let out a short guttural gasp, but he would not cease his stroking and only smiled with understanding, his eyes revealing how much he enjoyed watching her pleasure as his skilful touch made her tremble all over and pant with need.

'Please, Xavier—' Sophie gasped out on a juddering sigh, sinking to her knees in front of him.

Wordlessly, he loosened the buckle on his belt and stripped off his jeans. In moments he was naked before her. Lowering her gently to the ground, he eased her into position beneath him. Stopping to trace her cheek with one sensitive fingertip, he slid his other hand down her back, removing the thong.

He took her slowly, conscious of her inexperience, and after the briefest pause when she cried out softly at the moment of penetration, he settled into her deeply, inhabiting her completely, stretching her far beyond anything she could ever have imagined, moulding his body completely with hers until they were one. The intensity of sensation was something she knew at once could never be surpassed—then he moved again, and it increased. Withdrawing completely in one slow movement, he plunged into her again, and then again and again, until she was moving with him in an unbroken primal dance that only ended to begin again, for having found each other and waited so long they were like two parched creatures at the well of life.

It was almost dark when Xavier looked up into the sky again. 'There they go,' he murmured softly.

Lifting her head, Sophie saw the two huge birds swooping away across the valley until they disappeared from sight. 'Thank you for bringing me here,' she murmured, tracing the outline of Xavier's hard mouth with her fingertip. 'It's been the experience of a lifetime.'

'As I hoped,' he said wickedly.

'I mean the condors too,' Sophie reprimanded, smiling as she spoke. But then he drew her fingers into his mouth and began to suckle, and she was incapable of thought. It was incredibly erotic—but, as she reached for him again, Xavier moved away.

'Time to go, *querida*,' he said softly. But he seized her passionately and dragged her back to him for one last, lingering kiss.

Only here…only with him, Sophie thought, softening as Xavier's fingers meshed through her hair after he'd helped her to button up her shirt.

'Do you trust me completely now?' he murmured, kissing her before she could answer him.

As his hands moved lightly over her neck and shoulders, Sophie trembled with desire for him again, the shivers spinning down her spine weaving pulses of sensation that made her reach for him urgently. 'I've always trusted you,' she exclaimed huskily.

'Then perhaps one day,' Xavier murmured, holding her at arm's length so that he could stare deep into her eyes, 'you will explain why it has taken you so long to trust me not to hurt you when I make love to you?'

'One day,' Sophie promised, but he could see shadows already darkening the light in her eyes like a cloud moving across the sun. 'Has someone hurt you?' he pressed, his face full of concern, urging her to share the pain.

'No,' Sophie said quickly, swallowing hard as she turned her face away from him, 'not me.'

'Who then?' Xavier demanded softly, gently bringing her round and tilting her chin with his hand.

Sophie pressed her lips together and would not look at him. It was something she never talked about with anyone.

'Sophie?'

Staring sightlessly out across the darkening valley Sophie shivered a little, but she found it oddly comforting that the little pocket of human emotion could nestle beneath a crag whilst nature played out its own drama on a much vaster scale. It changed her perspective and made keeping the pain locked inside her seem pointless. Turning back to look into Xavier's face again, she knew he would not press her for details, that wasn't his way. But hadn't she trusted him already with her body, her spirit, her very essence…? Couldn't she trust him with this too?

'I was frightened because—' She stopped, concerned suddenly that the words had been locked inside her for too long. Maybe she couldn't get them out—but the steady beat of his heart against her chest urged her to try.

'My mother…my mother was hurt,' she told him finally in a dry voice stripped of emotion. 'Often…many, many times…hospital…never honest about what happened…' She was speaking quickly now, the words choking out on dry, gulping sobs. But she had to get it over with—had to brandish the malevolence in front of Xavier, and challenge him to want her, now he knew the truth about her father was even worse than he could possibly have imagined.

When every painful memory had finally drained from her, she was left shaking and spent. But, instead of rejecting her, turning cold as she had feared, Xavier planted tender kisses on her face and her eyes and her lips, while he stroked down the length of her shuddering back until, very slowly, she relaxed again and rested against him.

'Come,' he said when she had been still for a while, 'we should be going.' And as he pulled her to her feet, Sophie realised that the sun had dipped down low behind the peaks, casting a crimson mantle across the plain spread out below them. 'I'm sorry. I didn't mean to burden you—'

'Don't,' Xavier murmured, putting his finger over her lips.

'I'm glad you did. I guessed some of it, and I've been waiting for you to trust me enough—'

'There's so much you have to do, you've got to pack,' Sophie broke in, affecting a bright tone. His expression was hidden from her in the deepening shadows and she felt sure the extent of her revelations must have been a shock for him. She could only guess at his feelings.

'Stop it, Sophie,' Xavier insisted, his voice full of passion. 'You don't have to be brave—not with me.' He dragged her close and held her until she relaxed against him. 'Better,' he murmured at last, cupping her face in his hands as he stared deep into her eyes. 'We should go now,' he whispered tenderly, 'or had you forgotten, *querida*, that you still have to pack too?'

As soon as Sophie saw Anna Groes waiting for them on the top step of the clinic her happiness evaporated. Problems never went away of their own accord—they only stacked up awaiting attention until you dealt with them, she mused grimly as Xavier drew the truck to a halt.

Anna seemed to be waiting expressly for them—perhaps she had been standing there on tenterhooks ever since they drove off! But, whatever the story, she looked pretty pleased with herself now. She came tripping down the steps to greet them with a broad smile on her face, as if she was positively thrilled by their arrival. And, predictably, focused all her attention on Xavier.

'Some more doctors have arrived,' she said excitedly before he even had a chance to climb down from the cab. 'They are waiting inside to meet you—'

'I was expecting some more doctors, Anna,' Xavier confirmed coolly, refusing to be hurried.

She stood back expectantly and was clearly frustrated when Xavier came around the other side of the truck to see Sophie safely out first. 'Have they eaten yet?' he asked Anna, one hand still resting lightly on Sophie's arm.

Sophie saw by the merest flicker in Anna's eyes that she

had noticed the possessive gesture and resented it. But she also saw that the glamorous Danish doctor rallied fast. There wasn't a hint of petulance about her. In fact, Sophie decided curiously, she looked distinctly smug.

'I prepared a meal as soon as they got here,' Anna said with a degree of suppressed excitement that seemed at odds with the mundane revelation.

'Good,' Xavier said, walking alongside Sophie to the base of the steps. 'Well, we haven't eaten yet, so—'

'You haven't?' Anna said, tut-tutting with concern. 'Then I shall take the greatest pleasure in feeding you, Xavier,' she said, embroidering her offer with a flirtatious glance.

'Don't worry about us,' he replied pleasantly. 'Sophie and I will rustle something up.'

'But thank you anyway, Anna,' Sophie cut in with a quick smile. There was no point in fanning the flames of resentment when she knew that the medical world, like every other, was small and the chance of working with Anna again was high.

'Please yourselves,' Anna said, and this time she even gave Sophie the benefit of her perfect smile.

Sophie noticed some figures in silhouette, milling about behind the carelessly drawn curtains. The new doctors, she supposed. She was curious to meet them.

'There's one extra doctor,' Anna revealed a little more forcefully, clearly peeved by Xavier's rejection of her offer.

'Well, we can certainly use all the help we can get, don't you agree, Sophie?' Xavier responded, turning to look at Sophie. 'Sophie?'

But Sophie wasn't listening. She was standing fixed to the spot, staring up the steps towards the open door.

'Are you all right?' Xavier murmured discreetly.

Mutely, Sophie shook her head from side to side.

'Sophie!' The well-bred voice was distinctive, unmistakable.

Swallowing back her surprise, Sophie pinned a smile to her face. 'Henry. What on earth are you doing here?'

CHAPTER EIGHT

'I'VE come to see my fiancée, of course—what else?' Henry Whitland proclaimed as if that fact should be obvious.

Fiancée? Sophie's mind locked in surprise. Since when? But then she noticed his words were slurring slightly. Exhausting journey, free drinks, Anna's hospitality—there were always plenty of cold beers in the fridge. Whatever the cause, the effects were sure to have consequences, and that knowledge sent a shiver of apprehension down her spine.

Backlit in the doorway, in all his neatly pressed safari-suited perfection, Henry exceeded her worst expectations when, opening his arms wide, he exclaimed, 'How are you, Sophie darling? Come and give me a kiss.'

Xavier answered for her. 'She's fine, aren't you, Sophie? She's doing just fine, Henry. Welcome to Peru,' he added, leaning forward to shake hands with the older man.

'Delighted to meet you at last, Dr Martinez Bordiu.'

'Please,' Xavier insisted, 'call me Xavier.'

Xavier knew it was all bluster on Henry's part, Sophie thought with overwhelming relief. To her eyes Xavier had never looked more handsome, or more in control. She felt her heart swell as she looked at him—the steady expression in her dark blue eyes, the firm set of his mouth, the strength of purpose in his expression.

'Xavier,' Henry amended, fracturing her reverie. 'Thank you for taking such good care of my fiancée for me—my little Sophie.'

As Henry tottered towards her Sophie stiffened with embarrassment for him. His speech had degraded to a babble but, as she reached out a hand to save him from more humiliation, Xavier held her back—and, to cap it all, she had

115

Anna's smirk of satisfaction to contend with as the elegant Danish doctor stood on the sidelines watching the scene play out.

Ignoring Henry's comments, Xavier continued to behave as if everything was completely normal, and Sophie began to feel reassured as he led her up the steps with an arm lodged protectively around her shoulders.

'Sophie is already proving herself indispensable,' he explained to Henry, unhurriedly walking her past. 'But it hasn't all been plain sailing, and I know she's very tired.'

Tired? Emotionally exhausted after revealing the ugly truth about her parents' marriage—beyond exhaustion in a physical sense. But that had been the most wonderful type of exhaustion possible—until this moment, Sophie reflected. She was acutely aware that she was still throbbing and swollen from their prolonged lovemaking, still aroused, and bearing Xavier's potent, very masculine scent over every inch of her body.

'Isn't that right, Sophie?' Xavier demanded evenly, as he guided her towards the door that led into her room. 'Shower, and then a rest,' he suggested pleasantly, as if he had nothing more than her physical welfare at heart.

'Yes. That would be wonderful,' Sophie agreed, shooting an apologetic glance over her shoulder at Henry.

Opening the door for her, Xavier gave her an encouraging little nudge but, instead of leaving her at that point, he followed her in and closed the door behind them. 'Would you care to explain what that was about?' he demanded in a low, hostile whisper. 'Or shall I just work it out for myself?'

'No,' Sophie protested softly, sinking down on her narrow bed to get away from him. The room was small enough, but now, with Xavier inside it—Xavier in a rage, inside it, the walls closed around her, giving her no place to go, no place to think. 'I thought I explained to you already—'

'I remember exactly what you told me,' he said coldly. 'In fact, I can probably repeat what you said, word for word: "I'm not engaged to Henry. I never have been engaged to

Henry.''' Xavier stopped abruptly. All he saw through the red mist of rage was her father's face—the same mock-innocent blue eyes gazing at him right now… And after everything Sophie had told him about her parents, the manipulative little bitch! Wasn't this the ultimate betrayal?

Making a sound of contempt, Xavier drew himself up so that his head brushed the low ceiling. 'Women like you disgust me,' he said flatly. 'I could have any number of them.' He paused a few beats. 'Do you think I want *any* of them?' His lips turned down in a Latin show of pride. 'And do you know *why* I don't want them, Sophie?' he continued mercilessly. 'Because all I'd need is a heartbeat to have them— that and a hefty bank account, of course,' he finished scathingly.

'Now just a minute—' Sophie exclaimed angrily, standing to confront him.

'No!' he flared, that one short explosion of sound driving her back down on to the bed again. 'You wait a minute,' he demanded passionately. '*You* wait just a minute after I leave the room,' he informed her in a cold, steady voice, 'and then you go and shower every trace of me off you. Then get yourself dressed and come and join us—me and your *fiancé*, Henry, for some polite conversation and some food. A few minutes of our time is the least we owe him after he's travelled such a distance.'

'So you believe Henry and not me?' Sophie said tensely, meeting his fierce gaze head on. 'If that's the case, you're not the only one who thinks they have been misled.'

Xavier made a contemptuous sound with his tongue against the roof of his mouth. 'Don't try and absolve yourself from this, Sophie. It's too late.'

'You're right about it being too late,' she said bluntly, 'but, as far as absolving myself goes, there's no need since I have done nothing wrong.'

'Then why has Henry come all this way just to see you?' Xavier demanded, his eyes like daggers in her heart.

'I don't know,' Sophie admitted, 'but he's here now and

when he's sober,' she said pointedly, 'perhaps we should ask him.'

Xavier tensed abruptly, and Sophie could see that Henry being the worse for drink was a factor that he hadn't taken into account.

'I'll leave you to get ready,' he said coldly, 'then I expect you to join us.'

'Oh, don't worry, I will,' Sophie promised, in case he had any misconceived notion that she was going to run away.

Firming her lips, Sophie waited a long time after Xavier left before getting up from the bed. Then, quickly selecting some fresh clothes from the narrow wardrobe, she grabbed her wash-bag and headed for the shower.

'I heard there'd been some trouble,' Henry said uncertainly, glancing at Anna.

The source of his information, Sophie deduced, not allowing her thoughts to show on her face. They were all sitting in civilised fashion around a dining table in the clinic. Four very civilised doctors, behaving normally as far as anyone outside their tense group might suspect, but within that tense group Sophie knew the conflict was all too real, thanks to assumption, mistrust, and suspicion.

'Trouble?' Xavier said with interest.

'Sophie's midnight ramble around the countryside,' Henry clarified, pulling his lips down in a show of wry acceptance.

'Actually,' Xavier said matter-of-factly, 'Sophie saved a child's life.' The speed of his defence took even Xavier by surprise.

'I see,' Henry said. 'Perhaps I have been too hasty in drawing my conclusions,' he admitted, clearly flustered now. 'But you are all right?' he continued. 'This isn't proving too much for you, Sophie?'

He was sobering up fast, Sophie realised. She could see he was genuinely concerned about her. 'I'm still learning the ropes,' she admitted, with a quick, hard glance at Xavier. But the expression in Xavier's eyes was indecipherable. For now he appeared happy just to drink his coffee.

'It's everything I want, Henry,' Sophie confessed softly. And that was the truth, she thought defiantly—personally, professionally, in every way—and if Xavier's Spanish pride wouldn't let him see that...

'Well, you certainly have plenty to occupy you here,' Henry continued, unaware of the undercurrents, 'and, from what Anna tells me, there's always the redoubtable Lola to keep an eye on you.'

'Lola's organisational skills are incredible,' Sophie admitted frankly. 'The way she handles the administrative work at several clinics is invaluable for the project. But I don't need Lola, or anyone else for that matter, to *keep an eye on me*, Henry.'

How many more times? Sophie wondered. How was she supposed to stay on the right side of polite, when Henry seemed to think she was incapable of doing anything without supervision? But then she caught sight of the humour glinting in Xavier's eyes as he watched her; he was enjoying this, she realised, tightening her lips in defiance. Xavier was content to let her stew in Henry's patronising assumption that she had the stomach for adventure as long as someone else held the reins. Flaring a glance at him, she encountered something else in his glance—something unexpected. Was he over it? she wondered. Did he believe her about Henry?

'More coffee, anyone?' Xavier said easily, getting to his feet.

Sophie felt as if they were connected by invisible strings. Every movement he made, every flicker in his eyes, impacted on her senses, she realised, drinking in the power in his body as she tried to pick up clues—read his thoughts.

'Anna? Henry? Coffee?' he repeated, while Sophie could only wish their two companions would conveniently disappear so she could hear Xavier's reassurances from his own lips.

'Thank you, Xavier, that would be most welcome,' Henry said. 'Sure you won't have another one with us, Sophie?'

'Certain, thank you,' Sophie said restlessly, flashing another glance at Xavier as she forced herself to be patient.

'Xavier tells me he is leaving tomorrow,' Henry said brightly, looking across to Xavier for confirmation.

'That's correct,' Xavier agreed, placing three mugs of freshly brewed coffee on the table and a glass together with an unopened bottle of still water in front of Sophie.

'And then?' Henry said pleasantly.

'Then back to Spain,' Xavier said casually as he sat down again.

There was no mention of her accompanying him, Sophie thought, staring fixedly at her glass. He might as well have dragged her heart out of her chest and tossed it aside. She had imagined he was laughing with her, but he was laughing at her. And what would he do in Spain—for the next month, the next year…the rest of his life? She turned quickly to hide the rush of emotion showing on her face.

'Don't look so worried, Sophie,' Henry said.

'Worried?' Sophie shook herself out of it and drained the water in her glass.

'I said, you mustn't be worried because Xavier is leaving tomorrow. I know you're new here—'

'Not that new, Henry, and I'm not worried,' Sophie said firmly.

'And no need to be,' Henry said warmly, 'because I'll be here to look after you.'

As he sat back with a gleam of satisfaction on his face Sophie very nearly choked on her drink. As it was, she spilled half of it down the front of her shirt. 'You mean you're staying?' she said incredulously.

'Of course—if Xavier will have me. There are plenty of new recruits for me to train.'

He was actually rubbing his hands with anticipation, Sophie realised, feeling her stomach clench in alarm. But she knew she must not retaliate. The project needed all the doctors it could attract, and Henry was a superb mentor as well as an excellent doctor. 'I'm learning all the time,' she conceded.

'Quite right,' Henry said happily as if she was making his point for him. 'And, to make sure that continues, I shall be here to keep an eye on you, until you feel confident enough to—'

'I'm confident now,' Sophie said firmly. Now he'd gone too far. Her heart bounced off the toecaps of her boots. The clinic was too small to work in it with Henry. It would be like being confined on a very small boat—no avoiding him, no escape.

She wasn't even conscious of the angry appeal for help she flashed up at Xavier, who had observed the exchange in silence. But as the shadow of a smile touched his lips the annoying prospect of being shipwrecked with Henry sank to second place in Sophie's thinking. How was she supposed to concentrate on anything when all she wanted to look at was that harsh, sardonic curve at the corner of Xavier's mouth? All she could remember, all she cared about, was Xavier kissing her, Xavier touching her.

'I think it would be great if you could stay for a while, Henry,' he said, jolting her out of the reverie.

Xavier was only playing with her affections, Sophie thought furiously as she realised what he was saying. Was this his way of exacting revenge on the Ford family? He had made a fool of her one way, and now he was finishing the job by consigning her to the role of trainee under Henry's tutelage.

'Your training expertise would be of inestimable value to the project, Henry,' he continued evenly.

Sophie knew that everything he did, every ounce of energy Xavier dedicated to Peru, was in tribute to his brother, Armando. How could she put her pride before that?

'Are you sure you have the time to spare us?' Xavier continued, training his perceptive gaze on Henry's face.

'I have the time.' Henry hesitated for a few moments before he spoke again. 'I wonder, Xavier... This is rather awkward for me, but as Sophie's boss—'

Sophie tensed automatically.

'I realise that, strictly speaking, you inhabit that territory now—'

'Yes?' Xavier said, his voice hinting at the first signs of impatience with anyone other than Sophie.

'I wonder whether I might have a moment alone with you, Sophie?'

Xavier glanced across at her with an expression of enquiry on his face.

'Of course,' Sophie said, knowing that if Henry had any concerns about her work it was better to address them immediately.

'Just a few minutes should suffice,' Henry assured them, getting up.

'Well, I have paperwork to catch up on,' Anna said.

Content to go now, Sophie deduced. She could see there was nothing to hold Anna now that the drama had dwindled to little more than a storm in a coffee cup.

Xavier stood politely as Anna left the table and then, directing his comments to Sophie as she went to join Henry, he said, 'I'll be right outside.'

'Henry,' Sophie said with concern the moment Xavier shut the door behind him. 'What's wrong?'

'Well, perhaps you could tell me why you're not wearing my ring,' he said harshly. 'That would be a good start.'

And, to Sophie's horror, he shot out his hand and grabbed tight hold of her fist.

As she exclaimed and pulled away, he let go of her. 'I don't wear your ring because it would be inappropriate to wear such a large and ornate piece of jewellery while I'm working,' she exclaimed, nursing her hand. 'But I realise how precious it must be to you, and I keep it safe.'

'I'm supposed to believe that?'

'That I keep it safe?' Sophie exclaimed softly.

'No!' Henry replied in an angry whisper. 'That you took

it off for the reason you claim. Living and working out here in such close proximity with a man like Martinez Bordiu—'

'Stop right there,' Sophie insisted, raising her hand, 'before you say something we'll both regret, Henry.' Moving away from the table, she tried to give them both a little space, but he followed her. And, when instinct drove her to the door of her room, he placed his hand over hers, preventing her from seeking out the only private space she had.

'I know Xavier's a lot younger than me, passionate—'

'Henry? Henry! Please, don't do this!' Sophie exclaimed as he closed in on her.

'But I have feelings too—'

'Henry!' Sophie had to whip her face to one side to avoid his clumsy attempt to kiss her. As she called out, the door swung open and Henry catapulted back.

Remaining with her face to the wall for a few moments until she heard him sit down again, Sophie remained silent. For a few tense moments no one moved, no one spoke. Then the outer door closed softly and footsteps crossed the room towards her. Backhanding the tears from her cheeks, Sophie sucked in a deep breath and turned around.

'I hope I gave you enough time?' Xavier said, his face a grim mask as he looked down at her. With a slight movement of his head, he indicated that she should return to the table.

'Quite enough, thank you,' Henry replied tightly, dabbing at his lips with a spotless white handkerchief as he sat down again.

'Sophie?'

'Henry and I said everything we have to say to each other,' Sophie confirmed steadily. And then, just so that neither man could be in any doubt, she delved into the depths of her jacket pocket and pulled out the beautiful antique ring Henry had given to her back in England. 'You really should have this, Henry,' she said, walking across to hand it to him. 'This is not the place for it.'

'Yes…forgive me, I can see that now,' he said, unable to meet her eyes as he took it back.

He couldn't leave Sophie to Henry's tender mercies after what he had overheard outside the door, Xavier mused grimly. He would just have to take Sophie away—put some distance between the two of them as soon as possible. But the more time he spent with her, the more he wanted her. And where could it possibly lead? If his mother learned of his relationship with a member of the Ford family, it would be a nightmare. But what choice did he have?

'I would be proud to join you here in Peru,' Henry was saying in reply to a question from Xavier. He shot an imploring look at Sophie. 'I've taken a sabbatical from my work to come to Peru. I'll do anything—'

Henry was basically a decent man, Sophie thought, but he was lonely and she'd played a dangerous game, not making her feelings clear to him from the start. She glanced at Xavier, a man who exuded testosterone from every pore. She felt safe working with him, and knew she would never feel safe with Henry again. And she had never loved Henry; she understood that now. But she couldn't help admiring him. Volunteering to work in a situation so alien to him, it had to be hard—and would only get harder once he was out in the field. But the project was more important than her own feelings.

'You could bring so much to the project, Henry,' she said encouragingly. 'And we'll be working together again,' she added, trying to sound happy about it.

'Ah—' Xavier interrupted. 'I'm afraid that won't be possible.'

'Why not?' Sophie said uncertainly. Was she to be sent home then? Mashing her lips together, she forced back her angry defence. This was a tightly run ship. She respected Xavier's judgement. If he really thought she wasn't up to the job—

'I need you with me,' he said simply. His face registered nothing as he waited for her response.

'But, Xavier, I thought—'

'I can't help what you thought, Sophie,' he said firmly.

'The point is, Henry's here now, and I can use you better elsewhere.'

Disappointment hit her square in the guts. There wasn't a trace of intimacy in his voice—no hidden agenda, no *double entendre*, just plain, unadulterated fact. He was referring to her work and nothing else, Sophie realised, trying not to care. She glanced at Henry, who smiled ruefully back. He had resigned himself to a life without her, a life that absolved him from springing to her defence. 'OK,' she said, lifting her shoulders in a small shrug. 'I'm here to work, Xavier. I'll go anywhere you want me to.'

'Good. I'm glad that's settled,' Xavier said with satisfaction as if he had tied up the last of the loose ends. 'Well, we'll have supper now and then turn in. We've got an early start in the morning,' he said, shooting a warning glance at Sophie.

'Henry,' he added, clapping his new colleague on the shoulder, 'how are you in the kitchen?'

'So, where are we going?'

Sophie knew Evie would have answered her question right away. But Evie had taken herself off for her annual break to Rancho del Condor when she had touched down, and Xavier was piloting the light aircraft back to Lima. Apart from telling Henry he would be leaving for Spain soon, Xavier hadn't mentioned where they were going, for how long, or why. Sophie had hardly seen him to ask questions: he was always busy briefing the new doctors who had arrived with Henry. And now Xavier was lost in thought, with an expression on his face that suggested he wouldn't welcome a distraction. But she had every right to know.

'OK, Xavier, so I know it's Lima,' she said firmly, 'but what are we going to do when we get there? What will my duties be?' she demanded, getting heated now.

'Buckle up for landing.'

'Xavier—'

'I need to concentrate,' he said with maddening calm, adjusting the bank of controls in front of him. 'We're on the final approach.'

'What are we going to be doing in Lima?' Sophie said again when they had landed safely and were taxiing along the runway.

'I've got meetings, interviews.' He shrugged.

'And what about me?'

'You're my second in command,' he said. 'You'll be my sounding board.'

'And you consulted me about this, when?'

'I thought you should have a proper overview of the project. It will help you to understand how I go about fund-raising, managing my own financial input as well as the awareness exercises I carry out with the media.'

'Like I said,' Sophie demanded tensely, 'when was I consulted about this? I signed up to be a doctor with the project, not to glad-hand the press.'

'Well, that glad-handing is what keeps this scheme alive and thriving. And if you're so short-sighted you can't see that—' Before Sophie could launch a counter-attack he warned, 'I'm not in the mood for this, Sophie.'

The temperature was rising sharply between them. It felt as if he didn't want her there—so why had he brought her, Sophie wondered. Right at this moment, taking on Henry back at the clinic had more appeal than struggling to build bridges with Xavier.

Though she tried to harden her mind against him, her body had other ideas. But at least her mind remained firm—firm-ish, she amended, watching Xavier's strong hands moving with such efficiency between the controls. Everything those hands had touched, stroked and pleasured throbbed now with an insistent pulse. And the knowledge that they would never touch her again was unbearable—frustration squared.

'That was a heavy sigh,' he commented.

Sophie reddened, wondering if he had a direct line to her thoughts.

He glanced across at her. 'Are you OK?'

'I'm fine, thank you,' she said, pleased that her voice sounded so even, so controlled—in complete contrast to the jangling disorder of her heart.

Being cooped up with Xavier in the small cabin for the best part of the morning was no antidote to the erotic meanderings of an off-duty mind, Sophie realised, easing position in her seat. She was still aroused, still incredibly sensitised from his lovemaking… Maybe she always would be, she hypothesized with a short inward smile. And wasn't that better than nothing? It was certainly far safer than the real thing as far as her emotions were concerned.

'I know it's been a long trip,' Xavier commented, 'but don't worry, it won't be much longer.'

A long trip was right, Sophie mused wryly. Coming to Peru had been the journey of a lifetime in more ways than one. It was such a pity her fantasies couldn't have remained intact for just a little while longer.

CHAPTER NINE

XAVIER took an entire floor at the Inca Continental Hotel in the centre of Lima. But Sophie soon discovered that the grand old building bore no resemblance to any five-star hotel she knew. If it had to be rated in stars, a whole constellation would have been closer to the mark.

'This is my room.'

Sophie made herself ignore the spear of disappointment that the idea of Xavier sleeping alone induced as he led her across a huge and magnificent room. An illusion of additional height had been lent to the magnificently gilded and domed roof above her head by a series of diminishing scrolls. The bed was dwarfed by the size of everything else, but it was the use of colour she found intoxicating. Turning full circle, she tried to take it all in before Xavier whisked her away— brightest coral and gold, deep jade and sky blue—and everything that could be gilded had been, so that with the addition of the vast chandeliers glittering over their heads the room seemed filled with light and brilliance like an earthbound celestial cabaret.

'If the furniture is moved it can be used as another ball-room,' Xavier informed her casually, as a uniformed man-servant appeared out of nowhere to open some huge arched doors for them, 'in addition, of course, to the larger ballroom in the main body of the hotel.'

It didn't take much imagination to picture the scene when it was transformed, Sophie mused, casting a last lingering look over her shoulder. There would be ladies in couture gowns, and the men...perhaps some of them would be in uniform. And an orchestra...yes, a full orchestra, she decided.

'Are you coming, Sophie?' Xavier demanded, bringing her to her senses with a not so discreet cough. 'I've got my first meeting in less than an hour.'

'Yes…yes, I'm sorry.' She walked briskly through the doorway where he was waiting, feeling his force field envelop her briefly. And then she was past him and entering another even more fabulous room. An experience like this was a once in a lifetime event, she mused, gazing around with naked appreciation. She wanted to take her time… savour it.

'This is your sitting room,' he said briefly.

'My sitting room,' Sophie repeated, straight-faced. Well, there were sofas—four of them—so she supposed the magnificent space was used for that purpose. In spite of the question mark hanging over her presence in Lima, she couldn't help enjoying this chance to observe a lifestyle Xavier took for granted.

'And this will be your bedroom.'

As Xavier held the door open for her, Sophie gasped. If she had thought his ballroom-sized sleeping quarters grand, then this bedroom was a real revelation. The walls were covered in ice-blue silk emblazoned with gold, and there was a canopy over the huge brass bedstead in the softest leaf-green colour. This was edged and tied back with a deep shade of rose and the bed-covering over the plump pillows and quilt was lilac, as was the stained glass decorated panel at the top of each high, arched window.

'I hope it's to your liking?' he murmured, leaving her to walk about the room on what she guessed must be a priceless Aubusson rug in shades of cream, gold and rose.

'It's a little better than your base camp,' Sophie said dryly. She saw his mouth quirk briefly before he continued the tour.

'Here's the bathroom, where you can indulge yourself while I'm in the meeting,' he said, flinging open another door.

'I thought I was to attend the meeting with you—to

broaden my understanding of the project,' Sophie said pointedly.

'Not this first meeting—it's private business. It has no connection with the project.'

'I see.'

'No, you don't,' he assured her softly.

Did he have to prowl around her like that? Sophie wondered as a *frisson* of awareness raced through her. However large the room—and this room was large—it felt as if Xavier inhabited every inch. There was no escape.

Rather than yield to the feelings stirring inside her, she pretended interest in an ornate centrepiece on a vast cabinet at the other side of the room.

'Is George Jones majolica one of your interests?' Xavier murmured, coming to stand within touching distance.

'It looks so right here, but it shouldn't, should it?' she murmured, catching sight of her own reflection in an ornate gilt-rimmed mirror. Xavier was standing right behind her. She only had to lean back a fraction…

'I don't know,' he observed softly. 'The splendours of nineteenth-century English earthenware seem quite appropriate to me in this grand setting.'

Even reflected in the mirror, his dark gaze was hypnotic. It seemed to penetrate every inch of her and fill her with heat. 'The colours are very beautiful…rich, and lustrous,' Sophie managed breathily. Running the tips of her fingers over the deep turquoise surface, she could feel all the tiny hairs on the back of her neck rising in response to him. 'Must you leave right away?' she murmured recklessly, a part of her hoping he wouldn't hear.

'Why, Sophie? Is there something further you'd like to discuss with me?'

Discuss? No. Remaining with her back to him, Sophie remembered they had only an hour before his meeting. 'Yes,' she said. 'If this is your last stop before you leave Peru, I'd like to know when you leave…and what happens to me when you do.'

The bluntness of her question surprised him. She was hoping for some kind of commitment, Xavier realised. He slipped his arm about her waist and brought her close. They made a pretty picture in the mirror, he saw with cynicism. In spite of all that had happened, there was an ease between them. He dropped a kiss on the back of her neck. They could have been man and wife.

He pulled back. Sophie had to be seeing the same thing. He couldn't let it go on. Even he couldn't be that heartless. 'I go back to Spain. You can come with me if you want, but Sophie—'

'Yes?'

Already she sounded wounded, Xavier realised, hardening his heart. Better to set her straight right now before he did any more damage. 'I can't offer you the long-term.'

'I know that,' Sophie said quickly. What was 'long-term' anyway? Long-term misery like her parents? In her heart she had been expecting him to say something like this. She'd even thought she was ready to hear it. How wrong could you be? Sophie wondered, closing her eyes tightly shut to stop tears betraying the true extent of her feelings for him.

'Don't look so tense, Sophie,' Xavier murmured, 'I want you here with me. That's all I want right now.'

And, in that moment, Xavier realised he was telling the truth. He also realised she would assume he only spoke the words to keep her as his mistress: an emotional down-payment on a very cynical arrangement. Averting his face, Xavier wondered if he had ever despised himself as much as he did at that moment.

'Don't tease me, Xavier,' Sophie said softly. His reflection in the mirror wasn't enough. She turned to search for the truth in his eyes.

'Who said anything about teasing you?' Xavier said tenderly.

Even his voice had the power to caress her, to addle her thoughts and make her doubt her own resolve, Sophie realised. But he could cut her out too, she remembered. She was in Lima to do a job, not to be seduced by her boss. Her boss! Why could she never think of Xavier that way? Why must she always fight with him as if they were a couple, when it would be so much easier to accept him as her employer and occasional lover as many women might have done? 'Why are we here, Xavier?' she said firmly.

'I thought I explained.'

'I don't think you did, not the real reason. And I think you owe it to me now—'

'I owe you nothing on the personal front,' he said abruptly, his eyes turning from sapphire to stone.

'Because of Henry?'

'No,' he admitted curtly. 'I smelt the drink on his breath when I sat with him at the table. And I think you got rather more than you deserved from that quarter. Henry's out of the picture as far as I'm concerned. If you had only explained your understanding with him to me in a way a man can understand—'

'A man like you?'

'Any man who is not prepared to share his woman would ask the same,' he said impatiently. 'I thought we were close enough for you to trust me. After all your revelations about your parents…the intimacies we shared—physical, emotional—' He stopped, seeing the tears in her eyes. 'Sophie—'

As he reached out to her, she pulled back. Xavier was surprised to discover just how much that wounded him. Something closer to love than his customary pride made him try again. He only meant to draw Sophie to him, to hold her close for a few moments, perhaps kiss her head to reassure her before leaving her to prepare for his meeting. But as his arms closed around her and he felt her trembling beneath his touch, all he could remember, all that registered or mattered, was how much she meant to him.

They shared a hunger, and something even more than that, he realised, as Sophie raised her chin to gaze at him questioningly. But it was hunger now that was consuming him— that same hunger that, however hard each of them tried to subdue it, only continued to grow. It had become an all-involving passion for him, the like of which he had never known before. Would he ever sate the desire? Throwing back his head in one last attempt to regain control of his senses, Xavier realised he knew the answer to that even as he swept Sophie up in his arms and carried her across to the bed.

Stripping the lilac silk coverlet away in one impatient move, he laid her down gently on top of the softly yielding pillows. He helped her to undress, then turned his attention to his own clothes, removing them quickly and in silence. There was no need for words as they came together in an embrace that shook them both to the core. Sensuously, skilfully, he led her towards the inevitability of total pleasure, drawing out the tormenting seduction to its fullest extent before time constraints made him bring it to a close. And then, nudging her thighs apart, he teased her with a few lingering passes before tipping her up to meet him and inhabiting her completely. Xavier groaned, feeling her muscles tighten around him, drawing him deeper, insisting he pleasure her until the warm, silken noose of her body became a hot moist place that sucked on him convulsively as if she would drain the last drop of life force from him before letting go. It was pleasure such as he had never known…thought-robbing, breath-stealing, sensational pleasure, at an extreme he could never have believed possible. They needed each other, and that need was equally balanced, he realised, drawing back at the brink to look down at her flushed cheeks and passion-dampened face. What he saw mirrored his own fierce ecstasy. He slowed his strokes, making them long and firm, relishing each shuddering cry that escaped her lips and the sweet pain of her fingernails as they raked across his shoulders when she called out for satisfaction. But he would not be hurried. This was an experience to be savoured, and savour it he would, until the fire became an inferno, and with a few firm, fast strokes he pushed her over the edge into sensation-filled oblivion. He held himself aloof to relish the moment as she cried out his name, repeating it over and over as each fresh pleasure wave claimed her. And only when she stilled in his arms and moaned softly with contentment did he increase the pace again and find his own savage release.

Sliding out of her was the hardest thing he ever had to do, Xavier acknowledged, knowing Sophie felt it too when she groaned a soft complaint. But people were waiting for him...deputations, politicians, cameras. He sighed heavily as she clutched at him, her eyes still closed against reality, dozing in the light, sated slumber from which he knew he could so easily wake her, so easily arouse her again. But he could not stay in bed all day even if he wanted to and, with one final kiss, he went to take a shower.

'How can you go when I still want you so badly?' Sophie murmured sleepily when he returned to her at last to say goodbye.

'We have all the time in the world,' Xavier promised, sitting on the bed for a moment to relish her beauty. 'And if I make you wait you will only want me all the more.'

'I couldn't possibly want you more than I do,' Sophie argued, toying with the buttons on the front of his crisp white shirt.

Reluctantly moving her hand away, Xavier settled her back, drawing up the silken coverlets. 'Sleep for an hour,' he murmured, dipping his head to kiss her brow, 'and then take a relaxing bath. I will have beauticians visit you...and a masseuse who will massage all your aches and pains away.'

'I think you just did that,' Sophie pointed out, purring like a kitten.

'Then you will feel even more relaxed.'

'If I relax any more I may not wake up until I leave Peru.'

'Oh, you will,' Xavier promised in a low, husky voice that made her slide her limbs languorously over the sheets. 'I'll make sure of it.'

Sophie spent a full half hour of luxury in a bath the size of a small swimming pool, soaking in scented bubbles. She only climbed out with the greatest reluctance when the telephone handily placed on a marble ledge rang to inform her that beauticians would shortly be on their way.

Viewing the grand salon with its comfortable sofas, dainty antique side tables, rotating globe on a stand and vast rosewood desk, complete with silver gilt inkstand, Sophie concluded it was hardly her idea of a sitting room—hardly her idea of an appropriate setting for beauty treatments either. But that hadn't provoked a flicker of concern when she had suggested it as a possible venue to the person at the other end of the phone. The bedroom contained far too many erotic images for her to consider having a massage there. Even though she had smoothed the sheets and pillow-cases until she hoped not even the maid would guess what had taken place, the whole room seemed to vibrate with sensuality.

Answering a knock at the door, she found two young girls wearing crisp white uniforms. A parade of men followed them carrying cases containing all the paraphernalia they would require, and yet more wheeled in a full-sized massage couch. If this was how the other half lived, Sophie mused, standing back while they got everything organised, she could get used to it very quickly.

Soon she was daydreaming sleepily about enjoying the same sybaritic exercise on a daily basis. There was little chance of that, she reflected wryly as the girls continued to massage her back. But she needed it, Sophie realised, frowning a little. She had had no idea she had so many knotted muscles.

She moved slightly beneath the increased pressure. 'Xavier?' The click of the door closing softly behind the two girls he had silently dismissed gave him away. Turning her head lazily, Sophie groaned with pleasure and sank back again on to the pillow as he continued to knead her shoulders. 'I should have known—'

'You have an hour to get ready,' he murmured very close to her ear, 'and then you're on camera.'

'What?' Sophie shot up, instinctively grabbing the towel to cover herself. 'What do you mean, I'm on camera?'

'As my spokesperson. And you don't need that,' Xavier said persuasively, removing the towel and tossing it aside.

'There's no time!' Sophie exclaimed, gasping as his firm hands cupped her breasts. But as she wheeled around to get off the couch somehow her legs caught around his waist... 'Is there?' she demanded huskily, gazing into Xavier's rapidly darkening eyes.

'What do you think?' he murmured.

'You wouldn't,' she said, breathless with excitement. There was something irredeemably decadent about indulging their carnal passions on a massage couch in the middle of a vast and sumptuously decorated room, while she was completely naked and Xavier impeccably dressed in his tailored suit.

'Don't you know better than to challenge me?' Xavier demanded, tossing his jacket aside and reaching for the buckle on his belt.

Sophie's first television interview went better than she dared hope—even if she was aware that the beautiful South American woman who was supposed to be questioning her preferred looking at Xavier, standing just out of camera shot.

Sloe eyes, doe eyes, dangerous eyes, Sophie mused, feeling vaguely threatened by the woman's obvious fascination. Xavier was devastatingly attractive, and Sophie was the first to admit she lacked the drop-dead lusciousness of the woman sitting across from her. But she was becoming increasingly confident that there was a lot more going on between Xavier and herself than just physical attraction. They were linked at the core in a way she couldn't yet fathom, but she knew it went deeper than even the sensational sex they enjoyed...and that would never have happened without Xavier, she reflected, as she sat waiting for the credits to roll and the floor manager's signal that she could leave her seat. She could never have trusted, never have given herself so completely to anyone but Xavier.

Thankfully, he appeared immune to the woman's allure, Sophie thought as he embraced her when the lights dimmed.

'You were fabulous,' he said, dropping a kiss on the top of her head. 'Thank you so much for that, Sophie. You don't know what that means to the project. The world has to see feisty young women out here—'

'Feisty young women?' Sophie teased softly. 'Is that how you see me?'

'Maybe,' he agreed with a crooked smile.

'So you're using me as a free advertising tool,' Sophie murmured, enjoying the teasing banter as their eyes locked briefly, intimately.

'I'll do anything I have to do to make the project a success,' Xavier said honestly.

Sophie turned to glance as the glamorous interviewer stalked off, high heels rapping an angry tattoo across the floor. Sophie frowned. She had wanted to thank her. The interview had been a useful tool for the project. And now the woman had stalked off before Sophie could say a word to her about a follow-up. The rigid set of the television presenter's back suggested she couldn't believe Xavier had chosen to be with Sophie in preference to herself. Perhaps she had thought she was in line for a private tête-à-tête with Xavier after the show, Sophie worried, feeling she'd handled things badly. A glance at Xavier told her he wasn't aware of the undercurrents.

Xavier told Sophie later over coffee that their stay in Lima would be an intense round of interviews and meetings, and that she would be required to attend some and not others. He said he couldn't give her an answer as to how long it would all take and only stressed the need to be flexible. After he had ordered a light meal for them both, Sophie tried again to find out about the future.

'I'll be here for a couple of weeks or so,' he said casually, 'and then I'm returning to Spain. What about you? Have you made a decision about what you're doing yet?'

Bewilderment and hurt flashed through her, dragging her down, sapping her energy. 'I'm not sure.'

'That's not like you,' Xavier said, frowning as he caught hold of her wrist and made her sit with him.

It wasn't like her to feel as if her insides were being systematically shredded either, Sophie reflected grimly.

'So, go on,' Xavier prompted, staring at her intently.

'I'll finish my contract in Peru, and then I suppose I'll return to St Agnetha's.'

'I see.' Xavier frowned. 'I could use you in Europe,' he mused aloud.

'As what?'

My mistress? Xavier got to his feet and began to pace about the room. Would she agree to that long-term? He was sure he knew the answer—but still, he couldn't bear to be parted from her—not for a minute, not now or in the future.

He had a great choice to make, Xavier realised bitterly. He could ruin his mother's life by being with Sophie, or Sophie's and his own by refusing the commitment they both longed for. As he turned to look at Sophie he felt sure the agony would tear him apart. If only she would accept the medical position in Spain, at least they might work together if nothing else. 'Apart from the same sort of thing you'll be doing here with me in Lima, I've got one or two future projects in mind,' he said with a shrug.

Sophie swallowed convulsively. Her throat felt tight and painful as she looked away. She could focus on nothing. She had been building castles in the clouds. Happy families, a future together—inwardly she made a sound of contempt at her own stupidity. 'I'm not sure I can go on with this,' she whispered hoarsely as her thoughts escaped.

'Go on with what?' Xavier demanded, taking hold of her arms to drag her to her feet.

'Us,' Sophie said, shaking her head.

'Us?' Xavier dipped his head to stare her in the eyes. 'What on earth are you talking about, Sophie?' His voice was low, but intense, and filled with a frightening level of passion.

'You, me…bed.' Sophie was forced to turn away from the intensity of his stare. 'It's just not for me, Xavier. I—'

'What?' he demanded in the same low voice. 'I thought it was very much for you.'

'*It*?' Sophie shook her head in astonishment.

'Stop this, Sophie!' Xavier warned imperatively. 'I couldn't make love to a woman as I made love to you if it meant nothing to me.'

'But how many women are there who mean something to you?'

Xavier pulled back. She could see he was shocked. She had touched something raw, something deep, something so much a part of him. She wasn't surprised when he prowled a few paces away before turning to face her again. His voice was cold now.

'I'm disappointed in you, Sophie. I can't believe you would even ask me a question like that. Would you prefer to go back to one of the clinics when I leave here?' He gestured around the room impatiently.

'Can you arrange it?' She longed for him to say no with every fibre of her being.

Pride blazed a trail across his face. 'Of course I can arrange it.'

Disposing of her was that easy, Sophie reflected angrily. She'd been used and cast off, it was that simple. Xavier had succeeded in his mission—to teach her what sex should be. And she had been an excellent pupil, nothing more. 'So what am I to you?' she exclaimed. 'Some sort of medical experiment?'

'What the hell do you mean?'

'I think you know what I mean, Xavier. The sex—' She stopped. The gesture she made was of bewilderment, defiance.

The pain in her voice brought him back to her in a couple of strides. She tried to fight him off when he took hold of her shoulders, and pummelled her fists against his chest when he dragged her close. Then she swore at him, whipping her face away when he tried to control her with a kiss, but he was so much stronger than she was, and only held her hard against his chest until she had no fight left in her and rested tense and angry in his arms.

'Let me go, Xavier,' Sophie said, her voice muffled and indistinct against the front of his shirt. 'Let me go, please. Let me get on with the rest of my life. There's no point in this.'

The minute he released her she headed for the door. She had no idea where she was going. She could hardly see through her tears.

When she reached the door she spoke again. 'I'd like to return to the clinic as soon as you can get me on a flight,' she said steadily, keeping her back to him.

'"No point in this!"'

Xavier was there, trapping her against the wall, with his arms outstretched like two steel ramrods either side of her head. And this time she didn't flinch. She knew him too well for that, Sophie realised. She knew with absolute certainty that he would never hurt her. She forced her gaze up to meet his. It was the agony in his eyes that surprised her the most—it threw her completely. It was the very last thing she had been expecting. Pride, yes. Scorn, yes. Anger, certainly. But real pain, real concern, the fierce distress of a man about to lose everything he cared about was the very last thing she had been expecting.

'Don't do this to me, Sophie,' he said in a voice shot through with passion. 'Don't do this to us.'

'I can't—'

'Can't what?' he demanded fiercely.

The air between them was charged with passion as their heated words echoed around them like fiery ghosts, forcing Sophie to close her eyes against the rejection she was sure would come. 'I can't stand the uncertainty between us,

Xavier…because I love you.' The words came so easily to her…perhaps too easily.

Xavier drew her to him very slowly, carefully, as if she was made of the most fragile porcelain and might break into pieces at any moment. 'I never thought I'd hear those words from you.'

'Don't send me away,' Sophie murmured against his mouth.

'Send you away?' he queried ruefully, his lips tugging up in the crooked smile that only made her love him all the more. 'That's the very last thing I want to do.' But, as Xavier held her to him, his eyes were full of pain. 'And would I dare?' he whispered hoarsely in a desperate attempt to revive the humour that always drew them closer.

'Oh, I think you might,' Sophie whispered, but then his lips claimed hers completely and she was beyond speech. And this time his kiss was long and full of tenderness and hope. They had climbed a new mountain, she thought, as Xavier deepened the kiss, and the view from the summit was extraordinary.

Two weeks slipped into three, and then four, as the demand for information about Xavier's project grew. Alongside all the meetings and interviews, a steady stream of volunteers arrived in Lima, taking up every spare moment of their time. Living with Xavier was a crazy roller coaster ride of passion and laughter and unrelenting hard work, but Sophie had no complaints.

One night in bed, when she was curled in the security of his arms, she noticed some inner thought prompting the lips that had so recently kissed every inch of her to such devastating effect to curve in a grin.

'What are you thinking about now?' she queried softly, easing position on the satin pillows to scan his face.

'How much I love you.'

'Well, that's all right then,' Sophie murmured, sighing with contentment as she relaxed again.

'And...I was wondering whether this might be a good time to broach my suggestion about you working in Europe when we leave here?'

'Bribery?'

'Job satisfaction,' he countered with a wicked grin, moving the hair off the nape of her neck so that he could kiss her there.

Sophie arched towards him when his hand found her breast. 'Would I get the chance to do much hands-on work?'

'Lots,' he promised huskily.

'That's not what I meant,' she chastised in the same teasing vein. 'So, are you offering me a job?' she said more seriously, holding his hand still while she sought the truth in his eyes.

'Yes.'

'Are you serious?'

'Why shouldn't I be? I can use all the good doctors I can get.'

'And is that all I am to you?' Sophie demanded softly, evading capture when he reached for her.

'It's a very important part of who you are,' Xavier pointed out levelly.

Sophie's heart stopped. She had only been teasing him...

'Would you work with me, Sophie?' Xavier continued, unaware of the turmoil his words had provoked. 'Work for the project in Spain: recruiting, managing, flying out here when necessary—combining business and managerial elements with all your practical skills? There would be proper training available—'

Disillusionment prevented Sophie hearing any more. Xavier had just offered her the chance of a lifetime as far as her career was concerned—but, on the personal front, he offered nothing. His professional endorsement should have pleased her, but all she could register was the fact that his plans for their future were confined to work. There was no long-term future for them—somehow she had to get that through her head. But there was still a choice to be made:

she could allow pride to stand in her way and tell him to stick his job, or she could grab the opportunity to advance her career and enjoy the personal side while it lasted.

As if reading her mind, Xavier said, 'There would be no need for anything to change between us, Sophie. Our relationship should survive working together. I think we've already proved that, don't you?'

His smile was dark and dangerous, the type of smile that only minutes before would have made her heart thunder with anticipation. But now, for some reason, she was filled with apprehension.

'And I'll find you somewhere nice to live.'

Sophie refocused incredulously. What was he saying? It was all she could do to stop herself screaming—at herself for still wanting him on those terms, as much as at Xavier for imposing them. But, however much she wanted him, she had to make a stand. Travel, variety, challenge, hard work—everything that went with the job she would accept, but she would not accept Xavier's offer to find her a home. It made her feel bought, as if he expected to pay for her services.

'So, what do you think?' Xavier pressed.

'The job's great, and I'm sure you pay well. I should have no trouble finding myself somewhere to live.'

'As you wish,' he said with a shrug. 'But you do accept my offer of a job?'

'I do,' Sophie said, pushing aside the regret that there was nothing more to the offer than that.

While Xavier attended his last solo meeting of that day Sophie began to study all the papers he had left for her to read about his various other projects and business interests. The opportunities for her within his group of companies were boundless. The chance to add a second language as well as a professional management degree to her existing qualifications held real appeal. It was customary, Xavier had explained, for all his employees to be given training opportunities. 'All his employees—' that phrase had stuck in her head, Sophie realised as she glanced at her wrist-watch. The chance to work for Xavier—in Spain, in Peru, who knew where next?—was a fantastic opportunity; why not leave it at that?

She had already discovered a state of the art television with satellite channels in the bedroom concealed inside an ornate white cabinet at the foot of the bed and, deciding to catch up on the news to pass the time until Xavier's return, she turned it on.

The first few items washed over her, but suddenly the stricken, mud-coated face of the person being interviewed drew her closer to the set. Turning up the sound, she listened intently. As the full import of what she was hearing struck home, Sophie tensed, her hand automatically reaching for the telephone on the nearby side-table while she kept her gaze fixed firmly on the screen.

'Yes…yes,' she said urgently to the English-speaking operator on the other end of the line. 'You must connect me to Dr Martinez Bordiu immediately.' She waited tensely for what seemed like for ever. 'No, I don't care how long it takes,' she said firmly when the man finally came back on the line. 'I must speak to him right away. It's an emergency. Yes, thank you. I'll wait.' She sat back, toying impatiently with the stack of papers she had been reading. Suddenly something she hadn't noticed before caught her eye. Slipped inside one of the glossy brochures there was a single sheet of crisp white paper. Written in a confident sweep of bold black ink across the top of the page was that day's date and, underneath that, Xavier's name—*Xavier darling*, to be precise. Sophie's mind sucked in and analysed every word on the page in one single agonised glance.

Don't forget our meeting this afternoon. I am lost without you, my darling.

*   *   *

To find his mother holding court in an elegant salon on the other side of the city amidst a coterie of admirers came as no surprise to Xavier. Señora Martinez Bordiu was imbued with a remarkable charm together with beauty and intellect that seemed only to have increased with age. Sometimes, Xavier mused, watching her from the doorway for a moment, he wondered if only he could see the deep wound that lay behind her remarkable eyes, the wound that even the passage of time could not erase.

Her laughter rang out musically above the animated chatter. Even the President was enraptured, Xavier noticed. A muscle flexed in his jaw. *Enjoy it while you can, my darling mother, for I am about to break your heart.*

The furrows in his brow deepened. The sound of the mobile phone in his pocket starting to ring was the last thing he needed at a moment like this.

'Xavier…Xavier, is that you?' Sophie heard his voice seeming muffled, far away—as if he was explaining the interruption. Of course, the person who had written him the note would be with him, Sophie reminded herself tensely. What else had she expected? But, whatever their personal situation, this was something he had to hear.

'Sophie.' Xavier's voice was terse and dry, leaving her in no doubt that he didn't welcome the intrusion.

'Look, Xavier, I'm sorry—'

'What is it?'

'You must come back here right away.'

'Out of the question,' he said flatly.

'But you must.'

'I can't. I'm not even at the hotel. I'm halfway across town.'

Sophie felt faint but she had to go on. 'Xavier, this is really important—'

'Look, Sophie, I just can't get away right now. I'm afraid it's impossible. I'll be back with you the moment I can.'

'No—' She was about to explain when another sound

somewhere in the background at his end of the line made her stop. It confirmed everything she had imagined.

'Sophie…Sophie, are you still there? Are *you* all right?'

'I'm fine.' The high tinkling sound of a woman laughing—the type of laughter designed to appeal to a man—called her a liar.

'Sophie? Sophie, tell me what's happened.'

'It's nothing,' she said, keeping her voice level. 'I can handle it.'

'Are you sure? Are you sure you're all right? I'm sorry, but this isn't a good time. I really have to go.'

I bet you do, Sophie thought tensely. The clinic in the mountains was being washed away by a freak flood, people were losing their homes, goodness knew how many injuries, or worse, were occurring—but nothing got in the way of Dr Xavier Martinez Bordiu's pleasure!

Instantly the image of the beautiful television presenter flashed into Sophie's mind and she made a sound of contempt for her own stupidity. No wonder they'd stayed over in Lima for so long! Hadn't Xavier said he would do *anything* to raise awareness of the project? Her lips were white with tension as she ran things over in her mind. The project had enjoyed more publicity than either of them had anticipated. No wonder! Sophie gave a short, humourless laugh. Had she really allowed herself to believe that the nightly slot on the news show with the lady in question was just a lucky break?

'I'll speak to you soon…the moment I can.' He cut the line.

'Don't worry, Xavier,' Sophie told the empty room. 'It's nothing I can't cope with.' In fact, she thought coldly, don't worry about anything ever again as far as I'm concerned. Just get on with doing whatever it is you're doing—I'll be fine without you!

As Xavier walked forward into his mother's salon, she felt his presence immediately and, rising from her chaise longue, proceeded swiftly through the semi-circle of admirers, moving across the room towards him with the unconscious grace of a dancer.

'My darling, Xavier.'

'Mother, I must see you alone,' Xavier murmured as they exchanged kisses, continental style.

'Why, of course, beloved,' she said at once, pulling back to search his face. 'So, what is it, my darling?' she demanded the moment the double doors had shut on the last of her visitors. Holding Xavier's tightly clenched fists between her own cool hands as they sat together on the sofa, she waited.

'I have fallen in love—'

'But that is the most wonderful news!'

'Is it, Mother?' Xavier said sardonically.

'But your face is full of pain,' she exclaimed. 'Tell me, Xavier, what is it? Is this woman married? Does her heart belong to someone else?'

He gave a short, ironic laugh. 'I'm afraid it's far worse than that.' He watched his mother's hand flutter to her chest, and knew the pain had already begun. He also knew he had no power to heal the wounds he must now inflict.

'Worse?' she gasped apprehensively, only confirming his worst fears. 'What could possibly be worse?'

Xavier steeled himself for what he must do. Changing grip so that now he was the comforter rather than the comforted, he held his mother's hands firmly in his own.

'I have fallen in love with a member of the Ford family—' As she tensed he felt a stab of pain to his chest as real as if his mother had used metal rather than the shared memories of Armando's death to wound him. But he knew he had to go on. 'I have fallen in love with Sophie Ford.'

'Sophie...'

His mother breathed out the name on a sigh, and Xavier was devastated to see the tears welling in her eyes—the tears he had inflicted. 'I am so sorry, Mother. If I could have stopped it...' He paused, examining his own feelings in an attempt to explain what had happened. 'But I love her so much—' He broke off as emotion thickened his speech.

They sat together in an emotionally charged silence, reliving the past, sharing each other's pain.

'But Xavier,' his mother whispered at last. 'That poor child... Poor Sophie—' She sighed heavily. 'How could you ever imagine that I would disapprove? Your father and I were always so worried about her—'

She broke off and shook her head, extracting a fine lawn handkerchief from the sleeve of her day gown to try and staunch the tears now running freely down her cheeks.

'Here, Mother, let me,' Xavier whispered, taking it from her to complete the task. 'Are you telling me you approve my choice of bride?'

She gasped softly. 'Your bride?'

It was as if the sun had touched her face with warmth...and when Sophie smiled it was as if the sun rose in his heart, Xavier realised, feeling a rush of emotion. But then something darker, something urgent, jostled for attention and he turned away to shield his mother from his thoughts. 'I think I may just have made a terrible mistake,' he murmured.

'A mistake?' his mother repeated anxiously. 'What are you talking about, Xavier?'

'I haven't made my feelings at all clear to Sophie. I couldn't risk hurting you,' he explained, switching his gaze to his mother's face. 'She rang me moments ago and I put her off...wouldn't speak to her. She was distressed—'

'You must go to her, Xavier,' Señora Martinez Bordiu insisted passionately.

'Mother?'

'If you have left her in any doubt, any doubt at all, regarding your feelings, you must go to her now,' his mother stressed anxiously. 'If you don't tell her plainly, after all she has suffered, after all she has seen in that sad, sad home, I fear you may lose her for ever. Sophie is a stranger to love between a man and a woman. Go to her, Xavier, I beg you—go to her now...'

*   *   *

Sophie reviewed her options calmly. Xavier was right to some extent: she *had* been fine—up until now, she realised bitterly. But all that was over, and for good. She'd heard the laughter. She knew what it meant. And, the fact that she'd been taken for a ride in just about every way possible hit home like a sledgehammer to the guts. Getting the operator straight back on the line, she asked him to put her through to the air service base Evie worked out of and, having established that there was a pilot available to take her back to the mountains, she called the operator again. She needed a taxi to the airport.

CHAPTER TEN

IT DIDN'T help Sophie's state of mind when she arrived at the airport to discover the small light aircraft had missed its take-off slot. Now she could do nothing but wait…and let her imagination run riot.

Determinedly, she blanked out all images of Xavier sampling various erotic delights with the television temptress. But as an hour ticked slowly past, all she could do was gnaw her nails with frustration. She was desperate to get back to the clinic where she was needed, and forced herself to accept that Xavier had let her go without a second thought. If he had cared at all, all he had had to do was ask the staff at the Inca Continental where the taxi had taken her, and he could have been at her side right now.

What excuse could he possibly have? Except that—as Anna Groes had so generously pointed out—Xavier was extremely highly sexed. She had been fooling herself into believing she was enough for him, Sophie mused angrily. Of course he was in bed with that television presenter woman. Who else could have been laughing so enticingly in the background?

When at last the small aircraft left the ground it was into an untroubled sky that gave no hint of the disaster Sophie knew was taking place just a few hours away. Shifting this way and that in her seat, she didn't even attempt to engage the pilot in conversation. He was content flying the plane, and that suited Sophie just fine. She could feel her agitation building with every passing minute. 'How much longer?' she demanded at last.

'We're nearly there,' he said, banking the plane. 'Can you see the runway in the distance?'

She could, and instead of it being deserted as she had expected, as they dropped lower she noticed a large cargo plane was already on the ground. And then she saw the line of trucks crawling like ants into the shadow of the mountains.

'Looks like someone got here before us,' she remarked, thankful that aid was on its way.

'There's an emergency plan ready to roll out at a moment's notice,' the pilot said, levelling up for landing. 'This is difficult terrain. Something like this is always threatening to happen. One phone call is all it takes now to set in motion a full-scale rescue operation.'

And she didn't need to ask from whom that call had come: Xavier. Xavier knew but he still hadn't attempted to come back to the mountains with her.

But why should he return when he knew there was no need? He was well aware that the delivery of aid was under control, because he coordinated it—and his expert services were clearly required elsewhere, she mused angrily.

As the X-rated scenes played out in her head Sophie couldn't think straight for a moment, but as she started to calm down she realised the cargo plane carrying aid was the reason they had missed their take-off slot. At least something was how it should be.

'I should have known,' she murmured, half to herself, half in answer to the pilot's explanation. She took another glance at the line of vehicles, clearly distinguishable now—a ragtag army of transport—even a bus. They would have come from villages like Agustin's: volunteers only too willing to take the aid Xavier had provided straight to the disaster zone. The smooth-running operation had his hallmark all over it.

Sophie's mood lightened when she saw Lola waiting for her in the truck, but when she started talking about Xavier as if he was the saviour of the region Sophie could only nod; her mind, her lips, her voice-box all refused to function.

'It could have been so much worse,' Lola chattered on happily as she leaned over the steering wheel to turn the truck into the compound outside the clinic. 'But, thanks to Dr Xavier, everything is under control.'

'Who's that man?' Sophie said curiously, hoping to change the subject.

'Which man?' Lola demanded, staring around as she wrenched on the handbrake.

The area was full of people, but everyone seemed to know exactly what was expected of them. The transfer of supplies from the ground to the vehicles waiting to take them up the mountain was being carried out with almost military precision under the direction of one man. He cut a purposeful figure as he strode about the yard.

'That one,' Sophie said, catching hold of Lola's arm as she pointed through the windscreen.

'Why, that's Dr Henry,' Lola said with surprise as if she couldn't believe Sophie didn't recognise him.

'Henry!' Sophie exclaimed softly. And it was, she saw as he turned around to acknowledge their arrival with a wave. She couldn't have been more surprised as Henry opened her door. What had happened to his comfy overcoat of flesh, his smug expression?

'Sophie,' he said, helping her to climb down. 'It's really good to see you!'

Any awkwardness between them sank beneath Sophie's amazement. Taking in Henry's weather-beaten face, the crinkles around his piercing blue eyes, she could hardly believe it was the same man. The businesslike set of his shoulders and the baggy, rumpled suit, which it took her some time to register was the same impeccable tailor-made outfit he had arrived in, belonged to a man who seemed to have found his true role in life.

Confirming this impression, when he escorted her inside she found the clinic buzzing with activity. Marcos, the boy Xavier had been tutoring, was there, working alongside Anna. And then she saw the teenage girl whose headwear had been decorated with a splash of vivid embroidery working with them.

'Angelina wants to be a nurse,' Henry explained, beaming at the young girl as he ushered Sophie off on the next part of her whistle-stop tour.

'There seem to be a lot more local volunteers,' Sophie observed, feeling a thrill as she looked around and saw the way everything was shaping up.

'More every day,' Henry confirmed, 'and several whom I am ready to recommend to Xavier for his training programme in Spain. He's made a real difference here, Sophie.'

'I know that,' Sophie agreed, forcing her personal feelings to take a back seat.

Acknowledging Anna with a smile, she was surprised to find it returned with warmth. There was no time to consider the change before Henry urged her on to show her what else he had been doing while she had been away.

'Xavier's sending more supplies,' Henry explained with pleasure, 'and he'll be arriving soon—' He broke off to glance at his wristwatch, unaware that the colour had drained from Sophie's face.

'Xavier's coming here?'

'Yes, on the next flight,' Henry confirmed. 'Surely you knew that?'

'I wasn't sure which flight,' Sophie fudged as emotion condensed in the pit of her stomach. She had no idea what Xavier's plans were—or who he would have with him. 'What do we know about casualties, Henry?' she said, forcing some steel into her voice to try and take her mind off Xavier's imminent arrival.

'We've been very lucky—no fatalities, and no serious injuries.'

That was the best news Sophie had heard. And if she focused on that—on her job, as she should have been doing all along—maybe she could even cope with Xavier. She would have to, Sophie realised, paying close attention as Henry continued.

'And those that needed more care than we could offer here at the clinic have already been transferred to the Armando

Martinez Bordiu Hospital. The damage is mainly structural. Some people have lost their homes.'

'Oh, Henry.' Whatever she thought of his behaviour on a personal level, Sophie knew his concern was genuine, and under Xavier's direction he had made a very good start on getting life back to normal for everyone as quickly as possible. 'You've come to care deeply for the people of this region, haven't you?' she observed softly.

'Yes, I have,' Henry admitted, ushering her outside again. 'And there's something else, Sophie. Someone else.'

'Henry!' Sophie exclaimed gently, 'I'm really pleased for you. Who is it?'

'Anna Groes.'

'Anna!'

'You don't mind?'

'Mind? Of course I don't mind.' Suddenly everything made sense. They certainly brought out the best in each other.

'Now, who's going to collect Xavier from the airstrip?' he mused aloud.

'Why don't I?'

'You, Sophie?'

'You've got everything under control here. I'd like to,' she said, softening her voice and hoping the venom didn't show in her eyes. 'Leave it to me, Henry.' If Xavier had brought the South American beauty along she wanted to be the first to know about it. 'When did you say Xavier's plane arrives?'

'I'm afraid you'll have to leave right away—still OK about it?'

'Absolutely fine,' Sophie said, mentally gearing herself up.

Fishing the keys Lola had given him out of his pocket, Henry handed them to her.

There was a certain irony in the fact that now it was her turn to be in the driving seat, Sophie mused, taking the truck to the limit of its speed. Recalling the welcome Xavier had given her on the airstrip just a few short weeks back, her adrenalin began to race.

But in spite of her bravado when she left the clinic, Sophie was taut with apprehension by the time the big cargo plane lumbered down the runway and drew to a halt. Xavier didn't keep her in suspense for long. He appeared at a door high above the ground and jumped down before the pilot even had the chance to cut the engines.

He seemed to be alone, but Sophie waited until she was sure. Apart from some more men and women she presumed were volunteers, there was no sign of television cameras and arc lights, or glamorous female presenters bearing microphones.

As if drawn by some sixth sense, Xavier swung around to face her and their gazes clashed. He started striding across the dusty strip towards her, closing the distance between them in the space of a few tense seconds.

'Xavier.'

'Sophie.'

'I'm surprised you could get away.'

'What are you talking about?'

'You're alone,' Sophie said, flashing a glance around just to be sure.

'Of course I'm not alone.' He jerked a thumb in the direction of the volunteers streaming across the runway towards the waiting vehicles. 'Why didn't you wait for me?' His voice was fierce with emotion, his eyes narrowed like arrow slits against the slanting rays of the early evening sun.

'I wanted to get back here as fast as possible,' Sophie said defensively. 'I thought Henry—'

'Henry?' He delivered the single word like a hammer-blow, looking shocked when she mentioned the other man's name. 'What does Henry have to do with this?' Xavier demanded tersely.

And then, before Sophie even had a chance to reply, he wheeled around and headed for the truck. Watching him climb into the passenger seat, Sophie realised she was so tense that her fingernails had carved painful crescents in both palms. But the job had to come before her personal feelings, she told herself, climbing into the cab beside him. 'I'll take you straight up to the clinic and fill you in as we drive.'

'I've spoken to Henry already,' Xavier replied, without granting her so much as a glance. 'He told me everything I need to know. So, if you don't mind, I'd just like to get up there as fast as possible.'

She had never seen him so edgy, Sophie thought, taking out her frustration on the door.

'When you've quite finished destroying my property, can we go?' he demanded tensely. He had underestimated her, Xavier realised bitterly. And he wasn't about to form a queue behind Henry.

Tight-lipped, Sophie started the engine. Xavier might have been back in his casual working uniform, but his face showed nothing but hard-edged pride. The message he was sending her came over loud and clear: Women didn't walk out on him ever—whatever the provocation. 'Well, get used to it, mister.'

'Get used to what exactly?' he demanded coldly.

Ignoring him, Sophie concentrated on her driving. She was relieved when at last they reached the clinic. She had every reason to leave Xavier, to scorn him, to hate him, but the tense, silent journey had served to prove nothing but the fact she wanted him as much as ever. She cared about him passionately, she still loved him—maybe she always would. But love wasn't enough, Sophie reminded herself forcefully. There had to be loyalty and trust too; without that, there was nothing.

Climbing out and scanning the yard, Xavier headed straight for Henry and she caught snatches of conversation. 'You're doing a great job…I couldn't ask for more—'

Joining them, Sophie envied Henry Xavier's approval for about a second before she remembered Lima and all that had happened there.

'Those extra tents you brought are just what we needed,' Henry was telling Xavier. 'You thought of everything.'

Xavier looked at Sophie, 'Let's hope so,' he agreed. 'Sophie will take me up to the site now.'

After Henry had given her directions Sophie found herself behind the steering wheel again. She kept her thoughts to herself and her gaze fixed exclusively on the road.

When they reached the point where the treacherous river had burst its banks the natural disaster took precedence over any personal concerns, and Sophie slipped back easily into her working role. She was as relieved as Xavier to see that most of the debris had already been cleared. Scores of volunteers were still busy working and a couple of the organisers were able to confirm that anyone injured had been taken already either to the clinic or to the Armando Martinez Bordiu hospital.

'It shouldn't take long for everything to return to normal at this rate,' she commented thankfully.

'You'll be surprised just how fast,' Xavier said as they walked back to the truck together. 'When you live with nature in the raw, seeking normality after something like this is all that counts. Timescales are condensed—people cooperate—and of course, Henry—'

Sophie stiffened. 'Don't.'

'Don't what?' Xavier exclaimed as he swung back into the truck.

Taking one last look around, Sophie climbed back into the driving seat feeling stronger. The brush with nature at its most unforgiving had put everything in perspective for them. Maybe she should have kept her mouth shut, but she didn't. 'What were you trying to say about Henry?'

'I wasn't *trying* to say anything,' Xavier pointed out coolly. 'I was merely going to say how thankful I am that he's dealt with everything so efficiently. It's good to know I've got someone like Henry on the team. Someone I can trust.'

'What are you saying, Xavier? Can't you trust the rest of us?'

'You were in a real hurry to get back here to join him.'

Xavier could feel adrenalin pumping through his veins as suspicion clogged his mind.

'You were in no hurry to leave Lima, Xavier,' Sophie countered, staring straight ahead. 'Or were the charms of that woman too great for you to resist?'

'What woman? If you want to stay here and work with Henry, just say so,' he retorted angrily. 'I'll keep to my own schedule and return to Spain. Then Henry can have a clear field.'

'There is no Henry!' How many times? And he had a nerve, accusing her when he had taken another woman to bed almost before their sheets had cooled. As Sophie stared across in furious disbelief, the brief distraction was enough.

The truck lurched violently to one side as first one wheel and then another lodged in a concealed hole in the ground. Yelping with alarm, Sophie braced herself to the sound of savage Spanish curses. There was a deafening crack, an ear-splitting screech of metal on metal. Two of the wheels lost purchase on the road altogether, and then the truck settled on to its side at an acute angle, so that briefly Xavier fell across her, trapping her under his weight against the door. With one last eloquent barrage of curses he pulled away and, grabbing the door, now above his head, swung himself out of the cab.

Crouching on the side of the truck he glared down at her.

'Don't even go there!' Sophie warned furiously.

'Don't move,' Xavier instructed harshly as she tried to climb out. 'The truck could roll on top of you. Let me pull you up.'

But Sophie was already feeding herself through the passenger side window, now just a few inches off the ground. 'Don't bother! I can manage,' she insisted, heaving herself through. Crawling commando-style on her stomach through the mud she waited until she was a good distance away from both the truck and Xavier before getting to her feet.

'You were lucky!' he exclaimed angrily. She was un-harmed. It was all he cared about. Xavier felt relief course through him as he viewed Sophie's mud-spattered face and clothing. 'Why didn't you let me help you?'

'Maybe because I could manage perfectly well by myself,' Sophie retorted, finding she was more shaken up than she cared to admit.

'Does anything hurt?' He started walking towards her.

'No, I'm not hurt.' Not physically, that was. 'Stay away from me, Xavier,' Sophie warned, backing away. 'I mean it. Don't come near me.' Making a few futile passes at the mud on her clothes, she glared him a warning.

'What is it with you?' Xavier grated.

'Me?' Sophie flared back.

Xavier made a furious sound to accompany his angry gesture. 'Don't I know it? You walk out on me without a word—'

'*I* walk out on *you*?' Sophie's voice rose again in barely suppressed fury. 'I can't believe you just said that,' she added in angry staccato bursts. 'The way I remember it, you left me at the Inca Continental while you went out on the prowl—'

'On the prowl?' Xavier queried, imbuing each word with his particularly cutting brand of Spanish pride.

'Don't pretend you don't know what I'm talking about,' Sophie said accusingly, squaring her shoulders as she faced up to him.

'I'm afraid I don't,' Xavier said, his voice taut like a bowstring. He came closer until every part of her was tingling with awareness.

'You had to leave me for a meeting.' Her eyes were icy. She refused to back down. 'I thought you were somewhere in the hotel. It seems I was wrong.'

'About a lot of things, Sophie,' Xavier observed coldly.

'Well, let's start with you!' Sophie insisted hotly. 'I don't have relationships with serial womanisers—'

'I'm delighted to hear it—I don't have relationships with women who sleep around. How could you think that plays any part in loving—?'

'Loving!' Sophie made a sound of contempt. 'You accuse me of sleeping around and talk about loving! There's been no one before you, and there'll certainly be no one after you. I've had enough of men for—' Something in his eyes made her stop. They were storm-dark with pride as he let her go.

'I have never accused you of sleeping around,' he said quietly, 'but I couldn't help but observe how keen you were to get back here to Henry—'

'I was in quite a hurry to get back here to see what I could do to help,' Sophie pointed out frankly.

Xavier made an elegant gesture with his hands, inviting her to continue, but Sophie turned her head away. 'I thought we had something,' she admitted softly, 'something really special. I was so stupid I even thought we meant something to each other—' She heard a break in her voice and stopped. For a few moments she didn't trust herself to speak. 'And then I heard that woman laughing—' Her throat felt bruised and dry as she fell silent.

'Have you finished now?' Xavier asked calmly.

'With you?' Sophie demanded tensely. 'Yes, I have.'

Why did that hurt? She was used to fighting her corner, not crumpling in defeat—was that why it hurt so much? She whipped her head away when he came a step closer.

'Is it my turn to speak now?'

'Please yourself,' she said, refusing to look at him.

'You heard a woman laughing somewhere in the background during our last phone call in Lima, right? Answer me, Sophie,' he insisted, catching hold of her chin and turning her to face him. 'That's why you stormed out of the hotel and caught the first flight you could back here. Well?' he demanded harshly. 'I'm right, aren't I?'

'I know what I heard,' Sophie said tensely, dodging the spear of his gaze, 'so don't even try to deny it, Xavier.'

'I wasn't about to.'

When she looked at him now her eyes had turned as cold as the blue water they had swum through in the mountain lake. 'Go on,' Sophie pressed through lips that felt like cardboard. She was filled with a need to have it over with and filled with dread, all in the same agonising moment.

'There was a woman in the room with me, laughing,' Xavier admitted. 'And no wonder she was happy—'

Suddenly Sophie knew she didn't want to hear it. 'Stop. Please stop,' she said, cutting him off.

'No,' Xavier said quietly. 'I won't stop. You have to hear this, Sophie, because I was with my mother. She was laughing because she had just concluded a very useful meeting with the President that will enable her to open a second luxury lodge downriver from Rancho del Condor. She was even happier when I told her that I was in love with you.'

'Your mother?' Sophie whispered, trying to take everything in.

'That's right, Sophie,' Xavier confirmed evenly, 'my mother. So perhaps now you would like to tell me why you came back here alone without giving me the chance to explain?'

'I saw the note—from her... I thought—'

'I don't think you did think,' Xavier interrupted coldly. 'If you had, you would have realised that I could coordinate a rescue mission far more successfully from Lima than I could from here.'

He loved her. Xavier had told his mother that he loved her... Hot and cold torrents raced through her veins as Sophie confronted the damage she had done to their relationship. 'I thought you were with the television presenter—and that's why you stayed so long in Lima.'

'I had work to do,' Xavier said flatly. 'As for being with anyone other than you—'

His eyes darkened with passion, making her remember that they had scarcely been apart for a moment except for when something to do with his work briefly intervened.

Sophie stared numbly at the damaged truck. She was good at breaking things.

'I want no one but you,' Xavier said fiercely, breaking into her thoughts, 'though sometimes I have to ask myself why.

Come here,' he said, holding out his hand to her as he tried not to smile. 'We're going to need a ramp to get out of here.'

He held up his hand when she started to speak. 'Did you hear something?'

'No,' Sophie said, staying still for a moment, 'I don't think so.'

'Yes,' Xavier insisted, steering his gaze into the trees. 'I can hear people talking… Stay here,' he said when Sophie made a move to join him. 'I don't need any more excitement.'

Perhaps he was right, perhaps there had been enough excitement for one day, Sophie conceded—for both of them. 'I'll wait. Don't be long.'

'I'll be straight back.'

While Xavier was gone Sophie distracted herself by collecting logs. But she looked up with relief when he came back. He was accompanied by a group of local villagers.

'They'll help us,' he said, 'but the light's nearly gone and there's not much more we can do until tomorrow. They're heading back to their village, and we've been invited to spend the night with them.'

'What did you say?'

'I said thank you. We don't have much choice—unless you want to spend the night here in the truck?'

'The village sounds really great,' Sophie admitted with a grin, dropping the logs she had been carrying behind the back wheels.

'Leave that now,' Xavier told her. 'We have to follow them—and they're in a hurry. There's a celebration in the village.'

'A celebration?'

'Full moon,' he said, pointing skywards. 'Fertility rites— a fiesta.'

'Which is it?' Sophie demanded, feeling her heart begin to race.

'Both,' Xavier drawled softly. 'Now's the time to change your mind if you don't want to come with me, Sophie.' He held out his hand and, grasping it, Sophie smiled up at him.

CHAPTER ELEVEN

IT WAS like being transported back thousands of years, Sophie thought as they approached the clearing where the ceremony was taking place. The primal rhythms, the colour and the haunting music, together with the heavy pall of incense overlaying everything, was like nothing she had ever experienced before. It was heady and sensuous...but while her attention had been captured by the colourful ritual she noticed Xavier's attention was focused on her face—and he was trying not to laugh!

'What?' Then she remembered she was nine parts mud to one part clean, and began swiping at her face with the back of her hand. 'OK, so I'm not dressed for a wedding.'

'You look great to me,' Xavier insisted roughly, removing some twigs from her hair.

'I do?'

'Pay attention,' he murmured, dragging her in front of him so that she could see what was happening.

But Sophie couldn't pay attention. She was hardly aware of anything other than the fact that she was pressed up hard against his chest, and it felt warm and right, and she could remember how it felt beneath her hands as clearly as if she was running them over him.

She grew alert again as a young man and woman as well as some elders of the village entered the clearing. They were all fabulously clothed and walked with the sinuous grace their centuries-old heritage had bestowed upon them. An air of erotic expectation hovered around the young couple, adding to Sophie's heightened senses. It was as if the drama in front of her melded with Xavier's charismatic presence at her back.

An impressively tall man conducted the ceremony. His

long black hair was crowned with a headdress of feathers. Carrying a staff of office in his hand, he wore a breastplate and leg armour harking back to some lost age, but made of stiff fabric rather than metal. His costume was richly decorated in blues, red and gold. The crimson and gold train that fell from his shoulders was borne by two younger men wearing floor length cloaks and feather headdresses. Behind them another carried a staff the height of two men, heavily ornamented with feathers—and heavy to carry too, Sophie deduced, judging by the grim expression on his face.

'Perhaps he's a thwarted suitor,' Xavier murmured in her ear.

As he dipped his head to whisper Sophie felt another loop of tremors bind itself around her dangerously sensitised body. 'Reading my mind,' she suggested softly.

The young couple were swaying slightly now in rhythm with some muffled drumbeats and the slanted glances they exchanged were full of awareness. The young girl's lightly dressed form was clearly visible beneath her ornate cloak as she moved, and her partner's toned torso showed the same bronzed, oiled perfection beneath his wedding regalia.

'What do you think of the clothes?' Xavier murmured softly.

'Lack of them, do you mean?' Sophie whispered back, turning her head a little. Their faces were so close…they were so close. Sensation was spinning a net of desire around her that made her want to sink right into it and forget everything else. She wanted Xavier to lower her down on to the soft ground so that she could yield to the rhythm of the drums throbbing through her.

'You may never get a chance to see anything like this again,' Xavier said, his warm breath so close to her earlobe she had to stop herself nuzzling into him to enjoy the rasp of the rough stubble on his face. Sophie made a valiant effort to take it all in. Vibrant costumes…men in reds and ochre, deep blues and white. Neat red hats, almost fez-like in shape. Women transformed into butterflies—richly embroidered skirts, vivid woven shawls and headgear. 'I like the pancakes,' she murmured dreamily.

'Pancakes?'

The regular pulse of his breathing was caressing the most highly sensitised part of her neck relentlessly. 'How do they keep them in place?' she managed weakly. 'Hats like pancakes…' As her voice trailed away, Xavier smiled.

'Are you losing it?' he suggested huskily.

'Yes.' And she was—losing control that was, willingly, thankfully.

'Shall I try and find out where we're sleeping?' he murmured softly.

'Yes…yes please.'

Taking hold of Sophie's arm, Xavier urged her away from the semicircle of onlookers and steered her towards the other side of the clearing. The accommodation some villagers directed them to was a small building set apart from the rest of the village. As Xavier pushed open the door Sophie saw the windows had been flung wide to allow the cool evening breeze to curl around the sleeping area. She swallowed as she looked at it. A vast raised area in the middle of the room, far larger than a conventional marriage bed, was covered in numerous throws, rugs and pillows in soft shades of madder, rust, coral and magenta. The only light came from a flickering oil lamp, and there was some incense burning in one corner giving off a soft and seductive scent.

A curl of amusement tugged at Xavier's lips as he looked at her. 'You're not having second thoughts, are you, Sophie?'

Sophie's breath caught in her throat as she looked at him. 'How long will we be here?'

'Just overnight.'

'And then?' She almost didn't want him to answer that. Now should have been enough…

'You know,' he said gently, resting his hands on her shoulders as he dipped his head to drop a kiss on the nape of her neck. 'Back to Lima, and then on to Spain. Why? Are you sick of me already?'

His eyes were dark, and the shadowy play of light on his features carved his face into a new, harsher image—one she felt wary of and drawn to all at the same time. 'Overnight's not too bad. I'm sure I can tolerate such a very small dose of you.'

'What do you think would happen if we increase the dose, Doctor?'

Sophie's faltering heart picked up pace. 'I…I don't know,' she murmured, her gaze locked on his. 'Would it be safe?'

'I'm not sure,' Xavier said huskily, running the palms of his hands very lightly down her arms. 'I haven't completed my examination yet.'

'You haven't?'

'No,' he murmured, smiling a little. 'It's time to open wide and say ah, Dr Ford.'

As Sophie's lips parted to chastise him he claimed her mouth with a fierce, possessive hunger and didn't release her until she was moving against him with the same desperate urgency. She knew she had missed him, she just hadn't known how much. She could never have anticipated the climax that overtook her—that made his arms drag her close to support her when her legs weakened beneath her. Throwing her head back, she cried out, first in surprise and then in ecstasy as the violent spasms rippled through her in an intense rhythmical sequence that seemed without end.

Kissing her and soothing her, Xavier murmured to her constantly in Spanish, the heat in his words intensifying her pleasure—passionate words of encouragement as he watched the waves of enjoyment consume her, and then finally, when she had quietened, much gentler words of love. 'Remind me to rethink my examination techniques,' he teased huskily against her mouth. 'Anyone would think you'd had to wait a long time for that.'

'I have,' Sophie complained softly. 'Almost a day.'

'As long as that?' he murmured wryly. 'Then I shall have to make sure you never have to wait so long again. But first—'

'What?'

'A bath, I think. You're still covered in mud, *querida*, and, much as I would like to lick every inch of your body, a bath would bring us both so much pleasure—'

'Can we?'

'Oh, I think so,' Xavier confirmed, leading her by the hand to some doors that led out on to a small clearing. 'When I was asked by the villagers what we would like—what they could do for us to bring us pleasure, I thought of only one thing.'

Following his gesture, Sophie saw a large tin bath on a raised platform. And the water was warm, she discovered, dabbling her fingers into its fragrant depths, and there were flower petals floating on the surface of the water...

'Big enough for two?' Xavier commented, breaking into her mental meanderings.

'I hope so,' Sophie said, turning to look up at him.

'Do you want me to take them off for you?'

'What? Oh...' Her voice broke on a sigh as he began removing her clothes, his strong fingers brushing her sensitised skin, tantalising her beyond reason. She shivered with delight when at last he came to the tiny thong she was wearing and she stepped out of it.

Lifting her in his arms, Xavier carefully lowered her into the bath, and then, stripping off his own clothes, he joined her at the facing end. Leaning forward, he dragged her close so that her legs were parted wide and secured around his waist. Then, cupping her breasts in each hand, he chafed each blatantly erect nipple with his hard thumb pads, chafed them with remorseless intent as he stared deep into her eyes, enjoying the pleasure he saw reflected there.

Sophie's breath came on a soft groan of surprise and delight. It was as if none of her needs had ever been answered before by him—as if her hunger had returned refreshed, unsated and redoubled. She needed him like never before; needed the touch of his knowing hands and the tug of his probing fingers, the nip of his strong, white teeth and the relentless purpose of his tongue when he lodged first one nipple and then the next against the firm roof of his mouth and began to suckle. She needed it all…all at the same time. Now. Letting out a long, ragged sigh, she admitted huskily, 'I've missed you so much.'

'And I you,' Xavier admitted, pausing to stare at her. 'You're quite right—a day is far, far too long…especially when you have the most spectacular breasts—' Lifting them gently, he feasted his eyes on the blatant signs of her arousal so clearly reflected in the almost painful erection of each prominent rose-tinted nipple. 'You were made for this,' he promised, whipping her senses to a new height of awareness with his penetrating stare. 'Made for me,' he said huskily, bending to capture one pink tip very lightly between his teeth. 'Deny it?' he challenged, pulling back.

'I have no wish to deny it,' Sophie assured him, linking her fingers behind his head to bring him back to her again.

After a while, when her soft rhythmic moans told him that she was all sensation, he replaced his mouth with his fingers and watched her responses with fierce enjoyment as he alternately tugged and caressed. Sophie wasn't capable of speech any longer. Even breathing was more effort than she wanted to make—she was scarcely aware that she was panting just to keep pace with her heart.

'And now I shall wash you, prepare you—'

Could she take any more? Sophie wondered as Xavier's whisper connected with an inner ear that seemed to have a direct line to every erotic zone she possessed. And then, as he nuzzled his stubble-roughened face against her neck, she could only whimper in encouragement.

The touch of his hands brushing against her as he wielded the sponge was electrifying. He left no inch of her untouched. And then when he tossed the sponge aside she made no complaint when his arms tightened around her waist and he lifted her, cupping her buttocks as she held herself in the position he wanted, and then settling her down so very slowly until she was completely filled by him.

'That is the most incredible sensation I've ever experienced,' Sophie admitted softly, resting against him with her head buried into his shoulder.

'I've warned you before not to speak too soon,' Xavier murmured, lifting her again until he had withdrawn almost completely from the moist warmth of her clamouring muscles.

'Again,' Sophie urged him hoarsely, 'again.'

'*Cierto, querida,*' Xavier agreed, taking control. But he took his time and would not increase the pace as she wanted so that when the moment came for her, it was in a reason-dousing firestorm of sensation. She was hardly aware that he lifted her out of the bath, or laughed softly as he went to lay her on the bed.

'What happened to my bath?' she demanded groggily, reaching for him as he came to stretch out beside her.

'What bath?' he teased, seizing her fingers in his mouth to suck when she went to stroke his face. 'There's not a drop of water left.'

'There isn't?' Sophie sighed with confusion. 'How did that happen?'

'I wonder?' Xavier murmured sardonically, 'Like this perhaps,' he said, capturing her hands lightly in his as he mounted her. And this time he took her where they both needed to be quickly and efficiently, using firm regular strokes that had her bucking and crying out in surprised delight as she climaxed beneath him again.

'I can't believe it,' she murmured softly later when they were lying together looking into each other's eyes.

'What can't you believe, *amada*?'

'There was a time when just the thought of a man touching me was enough to make me flinch... And now this—' She raised her eyebrows expressively. It was about all the movement she felt capable of right then.

Pulling her close, Xavier kissed the top of her head. 'I can't bear it when you say things like that,' he murmured huskily. 'I can't bear to think I wasn't there to protect you.'

'But you're here now,' Sophie said, seeking a deeper place in his embrace.

'I want to show you in every way I can that love isn't about possession and violence,' Xavier said, pulling back so that he could look deep into her eyes. 'It should be something tender and beautiful between two people. Exquisite, sensational, fun—even boisterous—but never, never cruel, Sophie, never unkind.'

'You're kind,' Sophie whispered. 'Thank you.'

'Don't ever thank me,' he warned. Tipping her chin up so she was forced to look into his eyes, he said softly, 'You should never have to thank me just for being kind.' And then his lips cut her off before she could answer him, and his arms closed around her again and they were making love, so that she only cared for the moment, only knew that she wanted him, and that Xavier made her complete.

'What's this?' Sophie murmured later when she finally managed to tear her gaze away from the broad span of Xavier's tanned shoulders and the band of muscle across his stomach as well as all the other remarkable assets he had encouraged her to feast upon. The object that had briefly claimed her interest was a large earthenware pot resting on a low table beside the bed. 'Is it in case we get hungry?' she guessed, raising the lid curiously.

Xavier groaned with satisfaction like a big cat basking in the sun. Stretching out his gleaming bronzed limbs, he turned his head lazily. 'Not food,' he drawled sleepily.

'What is it then?'

'Perhaps the villagers thought you might need a little encouragement.'

'Encouragement?' Sophie lifted the pot and put it on the pillows between them. There was some sort of thick cream inside and a delicious aroma began to fill the room. 'What's it for if we don't eat it?'

'Roll over,' Xavier instructed, 'and I'll show you.'

With a last curious glance, Sophie did as she was told and rolled on to her back. She watched as Xavier dipped his fingers deep into the cream and them withdrew his hand so that she could see how it coated his fingers.

'It is edible,' he confirmed, licking his fingers with obvious pleasure.

Settling her head back on the mound of comfortable cushions, her hands indolently crossed beneath it, Sophie murmured, 'My turn now.' She licked it off appreciatively as Xavier brought his hand to her lips. 'It's delicious. I don't understand—'

'It's used to massage the bride on her wedding night,' Xavier informed her, his dark eyes mesmerising as they penetrated every inch of her, filling her with heat. 'To enhance sensation, to prepare her.'

'It's a bit late for that.'

'You'd be surprised,' he murmured. 'And it would be very rude of us to refuse such a gift when it's been left here expressly for our pleasure.'

'Do you believe in its properties?' Sophie said curiously.

'I'm not sure,' Xavier said, pretending to frown, 'but I do think we should conduct some clinical trials.'

'Xavier!' But it was too late. He had already scooped up a good portion of cream from the pot and was applying it to her body with firm, rhythmical strokes.

'The old rituals include a massage with a cream derived from a particular tree,' Xavier murmured, his voice strangely soothing, while his touch had the opposite effect. 'That sap is said to possess magical properties that enhance sensation.'

Sophie's breath caught in her throat. 'I think it's working.'

'You do?' he murmured, pausing for a moment.

Sophie's whole body was alive with sensation, but it was the erotic challenge in Xavier's dark gaze that triumphed over her scientific mind. 'Why shouldn't it?' she said softly. 'If they've been using it here for thousands of years, who am I to doubt it?'

'And is that your reasoned conclusion?' Xavier demanded, holding his hands away from her just to tantalise her all the more.

'I don't think reason has much to do with it,' Sophie admitted, dragging him back again.

'Was that good?' Xavier murmured much, much later.

Good? Good didn't come anywhere close to describing what she had experienced with him, Sophie realised. 'Stunning,' she admitted softly, rolling on to her back again. She had the satisfaction of hearing Xavier's sharp intake of breath. Would he ever have enough of her? She hoped not.

'Brazen hussy,' he murmured accusingly, stretching his length against hers on the bed. Not quite touching her, he rested his chin on one elbow and stared into her eyes while he traced the contours of her face with his other hand. Dipping his head, he kissed her briefly on the lips.

'Please,' Sophie groaned softly against his mouth, feeling desire flare inside her again.

'Please?' Xavier murmured, pretending not to understand—though his eyes told her he did, and only too well.

'You know what I mean…what I want,' she insisted.

'Don't be so greedy,' he cautioned in a low voice.

'But Xavier, I—'

'But what, *querida*?'

'Don't make me beg,' Sophie warned, only half-joking.

The suspicion of a grin tugged insistently at his expressive mouth as he trailed his fingers down over her neck and on to her shoulders and watched her quiver beneath his touch. And his eyes were dancing with laughter, Sophie saw, writhing in torment beneath his touch. 'I warn you—'

'You do?' He seemed even more amused by this last declaration.

'I can't… I won't—' Making a supreme effort, Sophie made a feeble attempt to get away, get up. If he wasn't going to—

'Where do you think you're going?' he growled, dragging her back easily, and securing her beneath his controlling weight.

'Nowhere apparently, so now what?' she challenged softly.

'Now this,' Xavier said huskily, moving down until he

could take one of her painfully erect nipples between gently questing teeth. At the same time he took possession of her other breast, gently tugging and rolling the twin of the first tight bud between his thumb and forefinger while his palms nursed and caressed her at the same time.

Sensation she had anticipated, but somehow he had raised the game; this was something else, something so extreme, so pleasurable—yet every time she managed to slip under his guard and move against him he allowed her only the briefest moment of satisfaction before gently holding her off…and all the while he was moving lower, lavishing kisses on her belly and then lower still so that finally she moved her legs wide for him in shameless invitation. When she rested her legs over his shoulders and his tongue touched her there, Sophie knew she was lost. All she could do was submit to sensation and allow Xavier to control the pace of their love-making. He was so skilled, so instinctive and perceptive that wherever he led she would follow, and whatever he wanted she would give to him.

As she cried out his name and begged him to come to her, Xavier moved again, lifting himself away until he could stare into her eyes. Then, seeing the trust and need reflected there, he took possession of her completely with one fulfilling and compelling thrust.

It was only when dawn's silver fingers entered the room that they returned grudgingly to reality. It was like waking from a dream, Sophie mused. After the sultry excesses of the dark perfumed night, the new day showed things up in a very different light. She had slipped back into her role as Xavier's mistress…and it was nothing more, she warned herself, however much she liked to fantasise about their future together. And Xavier was already pacing impatiently about the room like a tiger with a thorn in its pad, tossing the covers about as if the long hours of sensual indulgence between them had never taken place.

'What is it?' she said. 'What's wrong?'

'My wristband,' he said briefly. 'It's gone.'

Instantly alert, Sophie started searching the bedcovers. 'When?'

'I don't know,' he said harshly, raking his hand across the back of his neck. 'I felt a tug down by the river. Maybe then—'

'Shall we go back and look for it?'

'Not if we want to catch the flight back to Lima. The time-slot's non-negotiable.'

'Oh, Xavier.' Sophie reached out to him.

'Don't,' he said, turning his head to hide his emotion.

'But I want to help… I need to. I'm going to,' Sophie said firmly, putting her arms around him and leaning her head against his strong back as she waited for a response.

'I could have saved him—'

It was the faintest murmur she had to strain to hear.

'If I'd been a doctor at the time of the car crash, I could have saved him.'

'You don't know that. You can go over it as many times as you like, but you must know you weren't to blame.'

'It was my car—'

'And it was my father who dared Armando to take your keys,' Sophie interrupted in a low, firm voice. How could she ever forget? Rumours at the time had been so cruel and ugly. People had said Xavier must have given the keys to Armando, but Sophie knew the truth—knew it, and had lived with it as long as Xavier. Her own father—the bully who had almost ruined her mother's life, had tormented the wild young teenager until Armando had been persuaded to sneak away the keys to Xavier's powerful new car—a car Armando had had no hope of controlling.

She could still remember every detail of that awful day even now, Sophie realised, holding Xavier a little tighter as she replayed it in her mind. Roaring past the tiny cottage they had rented each year, Armando had raised his hand in ironic salute to Sophie's father, as Sophie had stood, uncom-prehending, with her mother in the garden. She could still recall slapping her hand over her mouth in absolute horror as the scene had played out in slow motion with all the inevitability of a film you couldn't stop rolling how ever much you wanted it to, and her mother's instinctive cry as she had reached out her arms in a gesture of impotent appeal towards the recklessly speeding car.

It had all been hushed up, though no one could make the consequences disappear, Sophie realised. And after years of abuse her mother had finally had enough. When her father had confessed his part in it during a particularly morbid display of self-pity, her mother was even more horrified by his confession than she had been by his treatment of her. And so the tragedy in the Martinez Bordiu family marked the end of her parents' marriage too.

Sophie's thoughts jerked back to the present when she heard Xavier murmur as if to himself, 'Armando could have been anything he wanted to be... He could have been a doctor too—'

'Xavier.' Sophie cut him off, instinct guiding her as she stroked and smoothed the harsh lines of his agonised face with tender fingers. 'Don't torture yourself like this. There's nothing you can do that will change the past, but you are doing everything in your power to make a difference to the future. You are building such a monument to your brother's memory. Armando will never be forgotten.'

'I must leave,' he said restlessly, 'with, or without his wristband. There's my training programme in Spain. It's no use offering to sponsor young people if there's no one to run the programme—'

Sophie allowed him to talk, only relieved he was looking forward, not back.

'I'm not going to stop you catching that flight,' she promised, moving away from the bed. 'And you'll find someone to take over from you here. I know you will.'

'Who will take my place?' he said, viewing her keenly.

'I think you already know the answer to that.'

'Henry?' he said, his eyes clearing as he looked at her.

'Why not Henry?' Sophie said, smiling back. 'He's a wonderful teacher and doctor.'

'And you, Sophie?' Xavier demanded, a harsh note sounding in his voice. 'What about you? What will you do now?'

Sophie's life force seemed to drain from her as she stared uncomprehendingly into his eyes. Did he still think she had a choice? Did he imagine for one minute that she could have given herself to him so freely, so completely, if there was even the remotest chance they would not be together always—and on whatever terms he chose to name? Her gaze slipped automatically to his lips, but she wasn't waiting for his kisses now; she was waiting for him to speak the words that would mean she could go on living...the words only he could say.

'Has Henry changed so much you want him back?'

That was the last thing she had expected, Sophie realised, when she saw the fierce Latin pride take possession of his face. 'Don't,' she protested softly. But Xavier's eyes were like stone and his mouth a flat line reflecting feelings so intense she knew he was having difficulty containing them.

'Then answer my question,' he said tersely.

'Of course I don't want him back! How could you even think such a thing? And he's with Anna now,' she said, her voice rising in protest.

'He is?' Xavier said, rubbing the back of his neck.

Exasperation took the place of her anger. Didn't men notice anything? 'I wouldn't want Henry back, improvement or no improvement—Anna or no Anna. I want you, Xavier,' Sophie said bluntly. 'And if you don't know that yet—'

It was as if all Xavier's tension drained away, and in the next moment something else, something equally fierce, took its place. And he cut her off in the most effective way, his lips demanding, his tongue clashing against hers in a primitive dance. 'Why do you want me?' he murmured, pulling away to brush her mouth with the lightest, most tantalising touch.

'Goodness knows,' Sophie teased, unable to keep the smile off her lips. 'Because you drive me crazy maybe.'

His lips kicked up in a wry answering smile. 'Good. I'm glad that's settled.' Xavier held her back and stared straight into her eyes. 'Now I'm in a hurry, Sophie, and you have a decision to make—are you coming with me or staying behind?'

'Can I get dressed first?'

He pretended to think about it. 'Only so I can have the pleasure of undressing you again when you beg me to.'

'Well, that's never going to happen on the aircraft,' Sophie said confidently.

'Really?'

'Yes, really.'

He shrugged acceptingly. 'Before we leave there's something for you in the bottom of that pot of cream.'

Sophie paused with her jumper halfway over her head. His casual tone gave her no clues. 'Oh?'

'Aren't you even going to look at it?' Xavier demanded, holding the pot out to her.

'Is this one of your jokes?' she said suspiciously.

'A joke? No. But there's only one way to find out.' Dipping his hand into the pot, he pulled out something that fitted comfortably into his palm.

So comfortably, to Sophie's frustration, she couldn't see what it was. 'What is it?' she demanded, peering over his shoulder.

'Don't you know?' he said and, when she went to prise his fingers apart, he closed his other hand over hers. 'Shut your eyes and I'll give it to you,' he promised.

She did as he said and he pressed a small hide drawstring bag into her hands. She found it contained something warm and hard. As she hurried to release the stone from the protection of its bag and tip it out on to her palm, Sophie gasped as she saw what she was holding.

'Well?' Xavier murmured. 'Do you know what it is?'

Sophie studied the rough green stone, hardly able to believe her eyes. 'It looks like an uncut emerald.'

'Correct. I didn't want to accept it at first, but the villagers insist it is a gift of pride—of honour.'

'For you?'

'For us. Sophie, what's wrong?' Xavier murmured, cupping her face gently between his hands and tilting it up so that he could look into her eyes.

'I was thinking about my contract...about how much work there's still to do here. About the people and how they need us—'

He dropped a kiss on to her lips, cutting her off. 'And I have made a promise to those people you mentioned to go back to Spain and be ready to receive their young people for training. Won't you help me with that, Sophie? I need you there. The people in these villages have come to love you, to trust you; they will be more likely to send their young men and women to Spain if they know you're part of the training programme.'

'I want to. I want nothing more, but are there enough people on the ground here?'

'More coming every day thanks to all the coverage we're getting from the media...thanks to interviews like the one you gave in Lima.'

'And my contract—'

'Is with me,' he insisted wryly, running the tip of his fingers down the mud-streaked shirt she had put back on, allowing it to lodge provocatively on a button. 'And anyway, I think it's time I saw you in a dress, don't you?' he said, moving the finger slowly upwards to trace the line of her jaw. 'A very, very pretty dress.'

'Still a sexist,' Sophie accused softly. 'And I thought I cured you of that.'

'Oh, forgive me,' Xavier said in a voice full of irony. 'I didn't realise you don't like shopping.'

'Shopping!'

'Ah, at last I seem to be getting through to you,' he murmured with satisfaction.

Sophie looked again at the stone in her hand. 'But this must be worth a fortune.'

'A gift of honour,' Xavier reminded her.

Looking at him, she understood. It was a gift made with pride, something Xavier could understand only too well. Back in their world the emerald was a precious stone, but here Xavier's skills as a doctor were worth far more. This was the man she loved, Sophie realised, looking into his eyes. This man, who gave the people more than his money; he gave them his heart. 'It's a wonderful gift, Xavier,' she said softly, looking at the stone again.

'I know,' he admitted, frowning suddenly. 'I tried to explain you might not want me—' He shrugged, his expressive lips turning down ruefully at the corners.

Sophie looked at him again. 'Want you?' she murmured faintly.

'Want to marry me,' he clarified, trying to keep his stern expression in place. 'Well?' he said impatiently. 'Do you want to marry me, Sophie?'

'Is that your idea of a proposal?' she said wryly.

'What if it is?' Xavier challenged.

'You'll have to do a whole lot better than that,' Sophie told him, but her heart was thundering in her ears and she could hardly breathe with excitement.

'In that case, Dr Ford,' Xavier declared, getting down on one knee in front of her, 'would you—'

'Yes, yes, of course!'

'You don't know what I was going to say yet,' Xavier pointed out. 'In fact, I was going to ask for some help with my filing—'

Sophie's happy exclamation was still echoing around them as Xavier dragged her back into his arms.

'So, will you marry me, Sophie?' he demanded.

'Let me think about it for a while,' she teased.

'Oh, no, sweetheart, not this time. I've got a plane to catch. Yes or no?'

'In that case,' Sophie murmured happily, 'you don't leave me much choice.'

When Xavier stopped kissing her Sophie let out a long, soft breath as she stared at the green stone glinting in her palm. Even in its uncut state it seemed to hold the vision of a people and the beauty of their land deep at its core. It was a gift from a proud people, and one Xavier thoroughly deserved... But there was just one thing more that could have made the moment perfect, Sophie realised, gazing at the pale band of flesh on his wrist. She longed to be able to return his brother's wristband to him safely.

As the sun rose higher over the mountains the truck was returned to their door, almost restored apart from a few new scrapes along its faded paintwork. There was one last quick visit to make to the clinic before they left for the airstrip and the flight back to Lima, and then they would fly on together to their new life in Spain.

'There will just about be enough time to collect up the rest of our things,' Xavier told her. 'It will be a fast turnaround.'

Now the emergency situation had been resolved almost all the medical staff were waiting to see them off. Lola came bounding up to Sophie while Xavier drew Henry inside to ask him whether he would consider staying on in charge of the facility.

'I have packed all your things,' Lola said to Sophie as she took her arm and drew her inside.

'You've done a wonderful job, Lola,' Sophie said, gazing around at all the plastic dumpers lying on the floor just inside the door. 'What are these?'

'Unclaimed possessions from the flood.'

'Can I look through them?'

'Of course.'

It was such a long shot, but it had to be worth a few minutes of her time, Sophie thought, glancing towards the office where Xavier was still in his meeting with Henry. Sending frantic mind messages for him to take a little longer, she began to root through the mud-caked objects, some of them barely distinguishable from lumps of wood. The chance of finding a leather band amongst all the tangled debris was negligible—who would have noticed it? And if they had, they would have concluded it was of no value, she told herself firmly, turning away. But then, for some reason, she went back again for one final look—and saw it. Seizing the band, she closed her fingers around it. This was something even more precious than the fabulous emerald, Sophie realised. As far as Xavier was concerned, what she'd just found was beyond price.

Xavier flew the small light aircraft from Evie's flight back to Lima where his private jet was waiting to take them back to Spain.

'Will you be piloting this plane?' Sophie's excitement at boarding a small and very luxurious private jet for the first time in her life was tempered by the knowledge that it was a long flight, which would only seem longer without Xavier by her side.

'Not today,' he replied. 'Why do you ask?'

'No reason.'

'I thought you would enjoy travelling in a private jet. I could always arrange for you to catch a scheduled flight—'

'Don't you dare,' Sophie threatened under her breath as the flight attendants stepped forward to welcome them on board.

'Dr Ford and I will not require anything during the flight,' Xavier said pleasantly. 'Please feel free to relax.'

Opening the door that led from the crew's quarters, he led Sophie into what amounted to a small private apartment.

'You weren't joking,' she gasped when she saw the size of the bed.

'Do I ever?' Xavier demanded, drawing her into his arms

as he leaned back against the door and locked it. 'This is going to be a very long flight.'

'I can't wait,' Sophie murmured, melting against him as Xavier's low rumble of laughter vibrated against her neck.

'Doctor, you can remove my clothes faster than anyone I ever met,' she chastened softly, as he swung her into his arms and headed for the bed.

'So—you let men undress you often?' he said sternly, lowering her down on top of it.

'You know the answer to that,' Sophie said, catching sight of the luxurious cashmere blankets and crisp linen top sheet just before they hit the floor.

'Do I?' Xavier demanded fiercely, tugging his shirt over his head and reaching for the buckle on his belt.

'Yes, you do,' Sophie insisted softly, gasping out loud as his mouth found her breast.

'Prepare for take-off,' Xavier warned, moving briefly when she linked her hands behind his head to increase the pressure. Then, controlling her with one hand, he ripped off the rest of his clothes with the other.

As the engines revved to a new pitch and the jet began screaming along the runway, Sophie tensed. 'Did I tell you I was scared of flying unless I can see out of the window?'

'No, you didn't,' Xavier admitted, holding back to look at her. 'And I regret, *querida*, that is not an option for you right now. But don't worry, I think I know the cure—'

'You do?'

'Yes. First you have to stop talking… And then… Can you guess what I'd like you to do next, Sophie?'

'Open wide and say ah?' she guessed.

Xavier gave a low growl of appreciation. 'You're a real quick study,' he complimented softly.

'I do my best—' She broke off, incapable of speech, all fear of flying dispelled as his hands slipped beneath her buttocks to tilt her up to meet him. With a soft moan of anticipation, Sophie wrapped her legs around his waist, welcoming the firm thrust with which he initiated their lovemaking.

Withdrawing completely, Xavier laughed softly when she begged him to continue, raking his shoulders with greedy fingers.

'You're a hungry girl,' he observed between kisses, pretending surprise.

'Hungry? I'm starving!' Sophie admitted, transferring her grip to his muscular buttocks. 'Now stop mulling over what treatment to give me, Doctor, and just give me whatever you've got until I feel some improvement in my condition…'

EPILOGUE

XAVIER had been far too generous, Sophie thought, staring into the looking glass. A week long shopping trip to Barcelona had resulted in a room full of new clothes, as well as the most glorious and totally feminine wedding dress from one of Spain's top designers. Cut low at the front, sleeveless and slim-fitting, it skimmed past her hips to flare out into a gauzy chiffon skirt, with a long train sewn with countless tiny crystals that twinkled in the light at her slightest move.

On her hair, grown a little longer now at Xavier's insistence, she wore his family's diamond tiara to anchor the filmy Swiss lace veil she treasured because it had been his mother's, and on her engagement finger the fabulous emerald he had taken to one of Spain's leading jewellery designers to have cut and polished for her.

'You look beautiful, darling.'

'Oh, Mum, I wish you could have been as happy as I am.'

'I am happy.'

'Are you? Are you really?' Sophie demanded, slipping her arms around her mother's deceptively fragile-looking shoulders.

Brushing some wayward locks of blonde hair off Sophie's face, her mother smiled proudly. 'How can I not be happy when I look at you and see what a wonderful young woman you've grown into?'

'So, you don't mind that I'll be living in Spain? You won't be lonely?'

Her mother made a scoffing noise, and though Sophie saw the emotion backed up in her eyes, she could see it was happiness. 'You're really sure?'

'Certain, darling. I've no time to be lonely—I'm on far

too many committees, and Xavier's mother has already asked me to accompany her on her next visit to the Rancho del Condor. And now, darling, it really is time for you to change into your going-away outfit. Xavier will be getting impatient.'

'You can visit us any time, you know that,' Sophie stressed, impulsively giving her mother one more hug. 'And as well as visiting the Rancho del Condor, Xavier has promised to take you to Peru to see the medical facilities on our next visit.'

'Will you stop worrying about me?' Sophie's mother said with an accepting smile, as she began to undo the cunningly concealed hooks and eyes on the back of Sophie's gown. 'I'm absolutely fine. You and Xavier should concentrate your efforts where they're needed most. There's a lot of people out there that need you both, Sophie. You know you've both got my blessing, so go to it, young woman!' With one final proud and loving glance, Sophie's mother left her to join the rest of the wedding guests waiting in the grand ballroom that linked the west and east wings of the Martinez Bordiu *palacio*, or their 'town house', as Xavier jokingly referred to the family mansion in Barcelona.

'May I come in?'

'Xavier, I didn't hear you.' Sophie wondered if she would ever get used to the sight of her husband, and the easy familiarity between them. It still sent a thrill straight through her every time she looked at him. And today he looked more devastating than ever in the dove-grey formal suit he had worn for their wedding, with a crisp white shirt to point up his bronzed skin, and the sapphire silk tie bringing out the blue in his eyes—eyes that were trained on her face at this moment with a look that suffused every part of her with happiness and desire.

He gently drew down the hand that had flown to her breast in surprise and took her into his arms. 'Thank you for looking so beautiful today, for being so gracious to our guests—and, of course, for agreeing to become my wife.'

'Will the day ever come when you stop teasing me?' Sophie demanded softly, seeing the glitter of laughter behind his dark glance.

'I hope not,' Xavier growled, playfully nibbling her neck. And when he let her go at last there was an irresistible intimacy and humour in his look as it tracked appreciatively over her.

She was still wearing the flimsy white lace bra and thong he had insisted on buying her to wear beneath the wedding dress now pooled at her feet. And they might never catch their flight to the tropical island he had leased for the duration of their honeymoon, Sophie realised, if he didn't stop looking at her that way. She knew Xavier was thinking the same thing that she was. 'There's no time,' she warned, leading him on at the same time with a flash of her eyes, and then melting into him when he kissed her again.

'There's something missing from that outfit,' he murmured critically, holding her at arm's length to look her up and down.

'I know. I've got it right here,' Sophie told him, reaching for the beautiful Peruvian shawl.

'Let me,' Xavier insisted, draping it around her shoulders. 'Now, go quickly and get dressed, or I can't be accountable for my actions and we will miss our flight. Don't look so disappointed. We've got the aircraft to ourselves, of course, and, as I'm sure you remember, there's a large and very accommodating bed in our private quarters...'

When they were on the point of leaving Sophie's rooms at the Martinez Bordiu mansion, she touched Xavier's arm to hold him back. 'Before we go, I've got something for you.'

'What is it?' he said, frowning a little when he saw her face had grown serious as she looked up at him.

'This,' she said simply, unclenching her fist to show him what she had been holding.

For a moment Xavier just stared at his brother's leather wristband. Then, taking it from her, he put it into his breast pocket for safekeeping. 'How can I ever thank you for this?' he murmured.

'Lola found it. I had it repaired for you. Won't you wear it?'

'I don't need to wear it now,' Xavier said as he took her into his arms. 'Armando is in my heart, and in everything you and I do in his name. And it was you who taught me that, Sophie. You showed me how to look forward instead of back. And, although Armando's wristband will always be one of my most treasured possessions, his real legacy lies in our partnership, and in each young person who comes to the Armando Martinez Bordiu Medical School in Spain to be trained.'

'I love you, Doctor,' Sophie whispered, standing on tiptoe to plant a kiss on his lips.

'And I love you more, Doctor,' Xavier insisted with a wry smile. 'To hell with that flight!' he added, sweeping her into his arms.

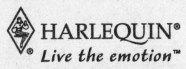

The world's bestselling romance series.

HARLEQUIN®
Presents

Seduction and Passion Guaranteed!

OUTBACK KNIGHTS
Marriage is their mission!

From bad boys—to powerful,
passionate protectors!

Three tycoons from the Outback
rescue their brides-to-be....

**Coming soon in Harlequin Presents:
Emma Darcy's exciting new trilogy**

Meet Ric, Mitch and Johnny—once three Outback bad
boys, now rich and powerful men. But these sexy city
tycoons must return to the Outback to face a new
challenge: claiming their women as their brides!

**MAY 2004: THE OUTBACK MARRIAGE RANSOM #2391
JULY 2004: THE OUTBACK WEDDING TAKEOVER #2403
NOVEMBER 2004: THE OUTBACK BRIDAL RESCUE #2427**

*"Emma Darcy delivers a spicy love story...
a fiery conflict and a hot sensuality."
—Romantic Times*

Available wherever Harlequin books are sold.

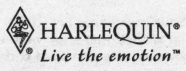

HARLEQUIN®
Live the emotion™

Visit us at www.eHarlequin.com

Coming Next Month

THE BEST HAS JUST GOTTEN BETTER!